Kindred Spirits: Ephemera

Jennifer C. Wilson

Read the complete Kindred Spirits series:

Kindred Spirits: Tower of London

Kindred Spirits: Royal Mile

Kindred Spirits: Westminster Abbey

Kindred Spirits: York

Kindred Spirits: Ephemera

www.darkstroke.com

Discover us online:
www.darkstroke.com

Join us on instagram:
www.instagram.com/darkstrokebooks/

Include **#darkstroke** in a photo of yourself
holding his book on Instagram and
something nice will happen.

To my wooden mouse.

About the Author

Jennifer C. Wilson stalks dead people (usually monarchs, mostly Mary Queen of Scots and Richard III). Inspired by childhood visits to as many castles and historical sites her parents could find, and losing herself in their stories (not to mention quite often the castles themselves!), at least now her daydreams make it onto the page.

After returning to the north-east of England for work, she joined a creative writing class, and has been filling notebooks ever since. Jennifer won North Tyneside Libraries' Story Tyne short story competition in 2014, and in 2015, her debut novel, *Kindred Spirits: Tower of London* was published by Crooked Cat Books. The full series was re-released by Darkstroke in January 2020.

Jennifer is a founder and host of the award-winning North Tyneside Writers' Circle, and has been running writing workshops in North Tyneside since 2015. She also publishes historical fiction novels with Ocelot Press.

You can connect with Jennifer online:

Facebook: www.facebook.com/jennifercwilsonwriter/
Twitter: www.twitter.com/inkjunkie1984
Blog: www.jennifercwilsonwriter.wordpress.com/
Instagram: www.instagram.com/jennifercwilsonwriter/
Amazon: www.amazon.co.uk/Jennifer-C-Wilson/e/ B018UBP1ZO/

Acknowledgements

Three of these stories were inspired by call-outs for collections, two of which were to raise funds for very worthy causes: Scoliosis Association UK and Newcastle Women's Aid. Writing these for a purpose made me think about a number of other places I really wanted to visit through the Kindred Spirits world, but which didn't necessarily warrant a whole novel. So, the idea of a collection of shorter stories was born, and I'm really grateful to Alex Marchant, Helen Hollick of Discovering Diamonds, Emma Whitehall and the other members of the Elementary Sisterhood for this.

I'm thrilled to be releasing this collection through darkstroke, and am so glad that Laurence and Stephanie Patterson enjoyed the concept of the collection. It's also a pleasure to be working again with Sue Barnard on the editing of the stories, helping bring everything to life.

Finally, a huge thanks to my parents for their help in getting information on some of the sites, and for their feedback on early drafts and ideas. There are a lot of places on the list which didn't make it into this collection, so there's plenty more 'research trips' still to come...

Jennifer C. Wilson

Cast of Characters

Sir Francis Walsingham (c.1532-1590): Principal Secretary to Queen Elizabeth I, controlling a network of spies in her service. Buried in Old St Paul's Cathedral.

Ursula St Barbe, Lady Walsingham (d.1602): Second wife of Sir Francis Walsingham. Buried in Old St Paul's Cathedral.

John of Gaunt, 1st Duke of Lancaster (1340-1399): Third son of King Edward III of England, and an established military leader. Founder of the royal House of Lancaster. Buried in Old St Paul's Cathedral.

Blanche of Lancaster (1342-1368): First wife of John of Gaunt. Buried in Old St Paul's Cathedral.

Arthur Tudor, Prince of Wales (1486-1502): Elder son of King Henry VII and Elizabeth of York, elder brother of King Henry VIII, and first husband of Katherine of Aragon. Buried in Worcester Cathedral.

Sir William Marshal, 1st Earl of Pembroke (1146/7-1219): Soldier and statesman, who served five English kings through a turbulent time in the country's history. Buried in Temple Church, London.

George Plantagenet, First Duke of Clarence (1449-1478): Brother of Richard III, father to Margaret Pole and Edward Plantagenet. During the Wars of the Roses, sided briefly with the Sixteenth Earl of Warwick against his brothers, Richard Duke of Gloucester (later King Richard III) and the then King Edward IV. Executed for treason at the Tower, reportedly drowned in a barrel of malmsey wine, and buried in the Tower of London.

John Donne (1572-1631): English poet, scholar and soldier, and ultimately Dean of St Paul's Cathedral. His memorial stone was one of the few to survive the Great Fire of London, and was re-placed in the new St Paul's.

Elizabeth I, Queen of England (1533-1603): The last monarch of the Tudor dynasty, famously choosing not to marry, leaving the English throne to the first of the Stuart dynasty, King James VI/I. Buried in Westminster Abbey.

Sir Christopher Wren (1632-1723): Architect, responsible for much of the rebuilding of London's churches after the Great Fire of 1666, including the new St Paul's Cathedral, where he was subsequently buried.

Richard III, King of England (1452-1485): The last of the Plantagenet Kings of England, took the throne in 1483, accused of murdering his nephews (the Princes in the Tower). Killed at the Battle of Bosworth in 1485 and hastily buried nearby, where his body lay undiscovered until 2012. He was reinterred in 2015 in Leicester Cathedral.

Anne Neville, Queen of England (1456-1485): Wife of King Richard III of England, daughter of Warwick 'the Kingmaker' (who played a leading role in the Wars of the Roses), and previously married to Edward of Westminster, son of King Henry VI of England. Buried in Westminster Abbey.

George Boleyn, Second Viscount Rochford (c. 1504-1536): Brother of Anne Boleyn, husband to Jane Boleyn. Executed on Tower Hill, accused of treason through adultery with his sister, and buried in the Tower of London.

Jane Grey, Queen of England (1536/1537-1554): The 'nine-day' Queen of England, Jane was a great-granddaughter of Henry VII, and was proclaimed Queen on the death of Edward VI. She was executed on the orders of

Queen Mary I, and buried in the Chapel of St Peter ad Vincula, Tower of London.

Margaret Pole, Countess of Salisbury (1473-1541): Eldest child of George Duke of Clarence and his wife Isobel, one of the final survivors of the Plantagenets. Executed and buried in the Chapel of St Peter ad Vincula, Tower of London.

Katherine of Aragon, Queen of England (1485-1536): Daughter of King Ferdinand II of Aragon and Queen Isabella I of Castile. First wife of King Henry VIII of England, mother of Queen Mary I, and the first female ambassador in European history. Abandoned when Henry wished to marry Anne Boleyn. Buried in Peterborough Cathedral.

Anne Boleyn, Queen of England (c.1501-1536): Second wife of Henry VIII, executed at the Tower in 1536 after being accused of adultery. Mother to Queen Elizabeth I, cousin to Katherine Howard. Buried in the Chapel of St Peter ad Vincula, Tower of London.

Jane Seymour, Queen of England (c.1508-1537): Third wife of Henry VIII, died after giving birth to the king's only legitimate son (later King Edward VI). Buried in St George's Chapel, Windsor Castle.

Anne of Cleves, Queen of England (1515-1557): Fourth wife of Henry VIII. Their marriage was annulled and she was awarded the courtesy title of "The King's Beloved Sister". She continued to live in England, becoming close to the future Queen Elizabeth I. Buried in Westminster Abbey.

Katherine Howard, Queen of England (c.1520-1542): Fifth wife of Henry VIII, executed as a result of her affairs before and during her marriage to Henry, including with Thomas Culpeper during her time as Queen. Cousin to Anne and George Boleyn. Buried in the Chapel of St Peter ad Vincula, Tower of London.

Catherine Parr, Queen of England (1512-1548): Sixth and final wife of Henry VIII, subsequently married Thomas Seymour (brother of Jane Seymour), who was charged with treason after her death. Buried at Sudeley Castle.

Sir Isaac Newton (1643-1727): Mathematician, astronomer, theologian, author and physicist, one of Britain's most famous scientists. Buried in Westminster Abbey.

Mary, Queen of Scots (1542-1587): Queen of Scotland, inheriting the throne at just six days old. Brought up in France, and married the Dauphin (later King Francis II of France). After his death in 1560 she returned to Scotland. Ended her days in captivity, and ultimately executed at Elizabeth I's command. Buried originally in Peterborough Cathedral, then moved to Westminster Abbey.

Claudia Severa: Wife of Aelius Brocchus, commander of a Roman fort along Hadrian's Wall in the first century. Writer of one of the most famous Vindolanda Tablets.

Sulpicia Lepidina: Wife of Flavius Cerialis, of the Ninth Cohort of Batavians, resident at Vindolanda on Hadrian's Wall in the first century. Recipient of a birthday party invitation from Claudia.

Richard Plantagenet, 3rd Duke of York (1411-1460): Great-grandson of King Edward III of England, one of the leading players in the Wars of the Roses. Father of Kings Edward IV and Richard III of England. Buried in Church of St Mary and All Saints, Fotheringhay.

Sir Henry 'Hotspur' Percy (1364-1403): Medieval nobleman and famous soldier, involved in a number of campaigns. Died at the Battle of Shrewsbury. Buried in York Minster.

Dick Turpin (1705-1739): An English thief and highwayman, executed in York. Executed in York.

Guy Fawkes (1570-1606): Key conspirator of the Gunpowder Plot of 1605. Born in York, executed in Westminster.

Saint Margaret Clitherow (1556-1586): Executed in York for harbouring Catholic priests at the Black Swan Inn; the manner of her execution (crushed to death under a heavy wooden door) shocked Queen Elizabeth I. Beatified in 1929, and canonised in 1970. A relic, her preserved hand, is kept in the chapel of the Bar Convent, York.

Peter Abelard (1079-1142): French philosopher and theologian. Most famous for his affair and marriage with Héloïse, and the subsequent scandal, along with their series of letters to each other. Buried in Père Lachaise Cemetery, Paris.

Héloïse d'Argentueil (c. 1100-1164): French Abbess, writer and scholar. Wife of Peter Abelard, famous for their series of letters, and considered an important person in the history of feminism. Buried in Père Lachaise Cemetery, Paris.

Elizabeth of York, Queen of England (1466-1503): Daughter of King Edward IV; wife and Queen Consort of King Henry VII. The only woman in England to hold the role of daughter, sister, niece and wife to a King (and mother, even though she died before Henry VIII took the crown). Buried in Westminster Abbey.

Edward IV, King of England (1442-1483): Son of the 3rd Duke of York, and elder brother of Richard III and George

Plantagenet. Buried in St George's Chapel, Windsor.

Elizabeth Woodville, Queen of England (1437-1492):
Wife of King Edward IV. Buried in St George's Chapel,
Windsor.

Charles Brandon, 1st Duke of Suffolk (1484-1545):
Brother-in-law and close friend of Henry VIII. Buried in St
George's Chapel, Windsor.

William Hastings, First Baron Hastings (c.1431-1483): A
close friend and courtier of Edward IV, whom he served as
Lord Chamberlain. He was executed on a charge of treason
by Richard III. Buried in St George's Chapel, Windsor.

**Mary-Eleanor Bowes, Countess of Strathmore and
Kinghorne (1749-1800):** A British heiress, with a
notoriously unhappy second marriage. The 3x-great-
grandmother of Queen Elizabeth the Queen Mother, and 4x-
great-grandmother of Queen Elizabeth II. Buried in
Westminster Abbey.

**Ranulf Flambard, Bishop of Durham; Roger Mortimer,
3rd Baron Mortimer, 1st Earl of March; William
Maxwell, 5th Earl of Nithsdale, and his wife Lady
Winifred** ("The Escapees"): A group of famous (or
infamous) individuals, all of whom have escaped the
confines of the Tower of London over the years.

**Elizabeth and Samuel Simpson, John Whatton, Marie
Bond, Susanna Peppin, John Westley and John Herrick:**
The spirits of people buried in Leicester Cathedral.

Claire [fictional]: Teenage daughter of a Beefeater, living
in the Tower of London.

Awen [fictional]: Regency belle, now barmaid of the
Barley Hall tavern in York. Friend and confidante of

Fawkes.

Kate [fictional]: Regency belle, friend of Awen.

Xanthe [fictional]: Receptionist and assistant at the Jorvik Viking Centre.

Detective Inspector Duncan Clarke [fictional]: Police officer, based in York.

Kindred Spirits:
Ephemera

Kindred Spirits:
St Paul's Cathedral

Present Day

The trio of ghosts stood before the grey tablet, reading (for at least the third time that week) the names inscribed there.

"To think," muttered Walsingham, "they had to use *that* spelling." The extra 'H' in his name had irritated him for over a century now. "I think I almost preferred it when they didn't commemorate us at all."

John of Gaunt and Arthur Tudor shared a look of pure exasperation. Sir Francis didn't think that now, and he certainly hadn't thought it then. Or at any point in the current cathedral's existence, come to that...

December, 1697

Walsingham, Gaunt and Tudor were standing in almost exactly the same spot as the memorial tablet would be installed, centuries later, although of course they couldn't know it at the time.

That cold December morning, all they could think about was how best to avoid John Donne.

"If he's insufferable now, just think what he's going to be like when the new intake begins to arrive," the old Duke said, looking at where the poet was preening, before making his way to the front of the cathedral.

"We have plenty of monarchs and nobles here from Old St Paul's; what makes him think he'll get any special treatment?" Young Prince Arthur turned to question his elders. "We three should take precedence over him too, I should imagine, today and going forward? I may not have been buried here, but I was Prince of Wales, after all. I would have been king, if I'd lived long enough."

The Elizabethan spymaster smiled at his friends, and glanced about. It was true; there were plenty of monarchs, courtiers, and other celebrated spirits in attendance, both residents and visitors. A lot of visitors. "Westminster Abbey must be silent as the tomb today," he said, chuckling at his own joke. "I was saying, dear, Westminster Abbey must be —"

"I heard you, dearie, I heard you." His wife Ursula rolled her eyes at him as she approached. "How many times have you told that to people so far today?"

"I've heard it five times at least," answered John, smiling as his own wife, Blanche, joined their little group. He looked across at Arthur. "Will Katherine be joining us for the ceremony today?"

Arthur glanced at the door. With Richard III having already arrived, escorting Anne Boleyn and Katherine Howard, it would certainly have been interesting, thought Walsingham, if Katherine of Aragon were to put in an appearance. He had already noted that Anne Neville, Richard's wife, wasn't with him, but then, not everyone was here yet.

"I don't think so," Prince Arthur replied. "I keep meaning to travel up to Peterborough, but what would I even say? I'm still hopeful she'll come and visit here one day. We were married here, after all: it seems the most sensible place to wait for her."

"Well, if it is meant to be, it will be," said John, clapping his hands together, clearly unwilling to share the young lad's worries, despite asking the question in the first place. "Let's get ourselves to a good spot and see what's happening."

What was happening was very much two events, depending on which side of the living / dead divide you happened to be.

For the living, this was a sombre occasion, as the great

and the good filed in, all keen to be part of the first service in London's great new cathedral. There was a heavy sense of anticipation amongst the congregation, and opinions on the design and décor were being carefully voiced in hushed tones.

For many of the dead, it was one step away from a party. It wasn't just Westminster Abbey which must have been devoid of spirits, as the dead of the Abbey, the Tower, the cemeteries and the dozens of smaller churches gathered. The streets leading to the new St Paul's had been teeming with life and death, with shivers unavoidable for the living, as the dead had no choice but to pass through them. At least, being December, most would be putting the sensation down to the cold, rather than any connection with their ghostly neighbours.

The party from the Tower had arrived first, with the Plantagenet brothers, Richard and George, now deep in conversation with Sir William Marshal from the Temple Church. As the myriad of monarchs from Westminster Abbey walked down the central space, most stopped to stare. There were plenty in attendance who had served under them, after all.

It was a reunion of sorts, then, and a situation which rarely happened in the capital.

Most of the ghosts had come out during the terrible fire of 1666, but that had been no time for celebration, and there was little any of them could do, besides ensuring some of the more heavy sleepers were awake well before the fire hit their homes. Today was, literally, a time to be joyful at the rebuilding of an icon. People could have fun, and they would.

But not everyone was full of cheer.

Donne's was the only memorial to have fully survived the devastating effects of the blaze three decades earlier, which had claimed the cathedral itself. Now, so many spirits found themselves drifting around the area, unsure whether they should move to another place, or, if they did so, whether they would lose their chance of gaining a white

7

light. Staying around on earth, whether at your burial site, or somewhere else which meant something important to you, was all well and good when you had a place to call home and a community around you, but for some spirits, that had now gone.

Some of the "Old St Paul's" crowd had made their way to other churches, hoping that a couple more spirits in amongst existing communities wouldn't cause too much trouble. Others had ventured further afield, returning to family homes to see what their successors had made of the place. But plenty were simply loitering, feeling misplaced and out of sorts.

"Once this is over, and the living vanish again, we're going to have to do something about these restless spirits," commented John of Gaunt, looking about the place. "The monarchs and most of the nobles are fine, but it's the more 'everyday folk' I worry about."

Sir Francis nodded. He had had similar thoughts, as the ghostly residents of the old cathedral hovered around. "I think the main concern is what will happen when we start getting new burials," he said. "I mean, there's really only Donne who has a place to call home. The rest of us, well…" His voice trailed away, as he realised that his concern was not merely for his neighbours, but for his friends, and even himself. Where would he and Ursula go now? It hadn't been so long since their deaths, that was true, but they had settled into a nice routine at St Paul's, and he wasn't sure he had the confidence to simply walk into another tomb, church or graveyard and make his presence felt. They were quiet folk, despite what he knew people had said about him and his role for Queen Elizabeth I.

"Look sharp," Arthur's voice cut through his thoughts. "My niece, and your queen, has just seen you."

Sir Francis and Ursula stood to their full height, ready to greet Gloriana herself. "Your Grace," the spymaster said, bowing as low as he could, given his age. "It is an honour indeed to see you here today."

Queen Elizabeth I extended her hand. Sir Francis bowed

over it, as his wife dropped a most gracious curtsey. "There's a good crowd out today, Walsingham," she said. "Any sign that there could be trouble?"

Sir Francis smiled, ever the courtier and servant to the Crown, even if the monarch currently demanding answers was no longer the one in charge. "We do not anticipate any difficulties, Your Grace. Although, as always, with so many people here about, and especially from so many factions, there may be disagreements, as would be expected, actual intentional harm to any ghost has not been heard planned in any quarter." He knew he must sound pompous, but it was true. Ever the spymaster, he had a network just as strong in death as he had in life, and they had all been paying extra-close attention to the rumours around London in the lead-up to the service. In the end, all he'd had to deal with had been the disgruntlement of the displaced residents.

Queen Elizabeth I nodded, briefly, before glancing around her. "It's impressive enough, but I'm not convinced on the style they are going for. I prefer the traditional feel of the Abbey. I'm certainly glad I shan't be relocated. Where do you see yourselves going?"

Sir Francis opened his mouth to reply, then Ursula stepped forward. "For the moment, Your Grace, we see no particular reason for leaving the current surroundings. It is pleasant enough for the moment, before our new residents begin to arrive, bringing whatever disruption they may. Although, as you can see, there is plenty of construction still ongoing, so I'm sure we can delay our decision for a little while at least."

"Quite, as my wife says," Sir Francis nodded. "I am hopeful that for at least some of us original residents, we shall be allowed to remain in place, and simply make the best of it, around the newcomers."

"There is no question of you being 'allowed' or otherwise, surely? You have the same right as anyone else to be here, and if you encounter any difficulties, be sure to tell me immediately. I shall see any issues remedied at once." Elizabeth looked around. "Any news as to who will be coming in, when it starts being used? I heard Donne was keeping his old memorial, and telling anyone who would listen about it whilst he was at it."

Sir Francis bowed his head to hide his smirk; he could see that his royal mistress was still as open to gossip and rumour as always. "A number of us are choosing to stay broadly out of his way, until he settles down again, my lady. He is, of course, rather enjoying his status, as the only one to have kept their original memorial."

"They are nothing but bits of carved stone; just remember that, my old friend," the queen replied.

"Easy for her to say, when hers is one of the finest in Westminster," whispered Arthur Tudor to Duke John, as they stood a little to the side.

Blanche gave him a stern glare. "That is no way to behave, young man. She may be your niece in the strictest sense, but she was still a crowned monarch, which you were not – even if you do still try to pull rank sometimes." She smiled over at Sir Francis.

He smiled back, having heard every word, and thanking his luck that he had always had far better hearing and observational skills than his queen. Now, their conversation over for the moment, Queen Elizabeth was walking towards the centre of the church, ensuring she had a prime spot for when the service began. It wouldn't be long now until the congregation was called to order.

At last the living and dead were all settled, and the service began. Although the Bishop of London's sermon, with its focus on Psalm 122 and its message about "the house of the Lord", gave everyone plenty to think about, it wasn't long before the dead were keen to abandon the formal aspects of the day and continue conversations they had begun earlier. Gradually, unseen to the living, the ghosts made their way out into the bright but weak December sunshine, wandering amongst the construction works which had been abandoned for the day to keep noise down during the service.

"An excellent service, don't you think?" Richard III was chatting to John of Gaunt, as Arthur Tudor once again loitered nearby. To his evident relief, Richard turned to include him in his question; clearly his animosity towards the boy's father did not extend to Arthur himself.

"Aye, not a bad preacher. Have you heard him before?" John asked, as the general post-service chatter built up around them.

"If you would have a moment, Your Grace," Walsingham sidled up to the last Plantagenet monarch, not feeling there was time for a natural lull in the conversation.

"Walsingham? Yes, what's the problem?"

"Well, I mean to say, this isn't entirely my problem to deal with, and I may be speaking out of turn in some quarters, but I'm aware, as I'm sure you are, that once the new cathedral is fully open, whenever that may be, well, there are a number of spirits who will be without any natural home. I wondered whether the Tower might have any capacity?"

Richard looked over his shoulder at the small contingent which had arrived from the Tower. "Well, we are quite busy, and you never truly know when others are going to turn up, but I'm sure we could take a few in, if it was needed. But I'm curious; this place has been gone, and being rebuilt, for years. Why now?"

John of Gaunt interjected. "I fear it was a collective error, on all our parts. We were, I suspect, naïve, in thinking they would never actually finish the new cathedral, or that it would at least drag on another couple of decades, even centuries. You know how long these things can take. Ask King Æthelred for one – he's been here since some of the earliest construction began on the site, and like so many of us, didn't see the urgency."

Richard nodded. "But now it's being opened, and potentially used, you're worried about the new residents, and how they might interact with you old guard?"

"Quite. I'm sure everyone will be nice enough to begin with, but you know how it is when new people arrive.

Everyone is a little fretted to begin with, and then there's the quarrelling. Just too much for those of us who have been settled long enough."

"I understand, of course. Well, let's say the Tower can take in, what, another dozen or two, comfortably. But they'll need to be of a suitable disposition. Able to handle a biggish crowd, the odd bit of haunting, and there's always plenty of comings-and-goings with prisoners, visitors and guards etc., both living and dead. It's not the quietest of homes to move into, especially not after a cathedral." Richard tilted his head, clearly thinking about how such a move would affect more calm and genteel residents.

"There is something else you could do, you know." The voice of Sir William Marshal interrupted their thoughts. "Sorry, I couldn't help overhearing."

Walsingham turned and greeted their group's new member. "Sir William, please, no problem at all. I know I'm hardly a leader in this place, but it appears my urge to control cannot quite be put down, even now. Please, do go on."

"So, there are, what, at least twenty of you left, now that a few have moved on, either literally or metaphorically?"

Walsingham nodded.

"Then stay. You're in residence, you have been for centuries, some of you. There are ancient kings in here, aren't there?"

"There are indeed," confirmed John of Gaunt. "Æthelred has been hanging around here since 1016, and showing no signs of wanting to leave, from what I can gather. Same with Sæbbi, and he goes back even further, to the six hundreds."

"Well then, get them to exercise their power a bit. Stand up for yourself, man, as a community, and show that you won't be moved on. Surely between you two you can rally the troops and get them to see sense? Also, with all due respect, Your Grace," he added, turning to Richard, "staying here will suit everyone a heck of a lot more than moving to somewhere like the Tower, however welcome you and the

12

others try to make them feel."

Walsingham didn't move for a moment, mulling over the knight's idea in his mind. It would certainly suit everyone far better to stay put, rather than trying to find homes where they might not be welcome. And even Queen Elizabeth had offered her support, if they found themselves encountering any difficulties. Could he and Duke John get everyone to agree, to stay together?

As though reading his mind, John turned to him. "If we can get everyone who's left to stand together, as one, then why not? How have we not seen this option?"

"Because, my friend, we have been so preoccupied with seeing the problems that we failed to spot the solution. I'm ashamed to admit, but I've failed us here." Walsingham looked to his feet, dismayed at having missed such an obvious response to the issue.

"Don't be a fool, man. Yes, a couple of folk have already left us, but who is to say they wouldn't have done so anyway, over time? But this, this we can act on now, and make a start. What's the plan?"

Walsingham smiled at the Duke, knowing full well what the plan was, and knowing that Gaunt knew it too, but was giving him the chance to take back charge. Not a bad gesture from a royal duke. Despite the nagging feeling that he should be insulted, instead he took the offer in the manner it was clearly intended.

"Right. Well, there's no point trying to do anything with so many visitors still present. I suggest we wait until tomorrow morning now, as I suspect there will be plenty of people staying on this evening, catching up with old friends, or possibly old enemies, but I rather hope not the latter. Let's send word around as best we can, without the visitors noticing, and get everyone to meet in the quire at ten o'clock sharp. From there, we shall make a plan."

Pleased with the way things had turned out, and secretly glad that he no longer needed to dispatch any spirits in the direction of the Tower, Walsingham moved on. His mind now awhirl with planning, always one of his favourite pastimes, he failed to swerve quickly enough out of John Donne's line of sight.

"Walsingham!" The poet raised his arm, giving the spymaster no alternative but to join him. "I see you left the service early, as did a lot of the others actually. Not the best way to ingratiate yourself to the new church community."

"Ingratiate? With whom, exactly? We were the only ones of the dead present. The place is nowhere near complete, and as a result, there shall be no bodies buried here at any point in the immediate future." Walsingham was already irritated by the man. "You are currently the only spirit with a memorial, but that doesn't make you the only resident. And even if you were, I'm not sure one person counts as a community."

Donne's mouth fell open. "Well, I mean, I, well."

"Ah, there you are, dearie. I was wondering where you'd got to." Ursula appeared as though from nowhere at her husband's side, slipping her arm into the crook of his elbow. "John, how are you settling in? Are you happy with where they popped your old memorial? It's so funny, everyone else wondering if we'll get shiny new ones elsewhere, to replace what's been lost, or where we'll all go, but there's yours, the old stone, still there. You can even see the hint of the ash, or is that just me?"

Walsingham grinned. His wife was a genius. Why hadn't he thought of things this way before: that Donne was being stuck with an old stone, whereas so many others might indeed get a new memorial? The look on Donne's face was priceless.

"At least they've managed to restore it to its former glory," Ursula went on, bestowing the briefest of smiles on her husband. "I mean, we wouldn't have wanted all that effort to go to waste. Not after you spent so long posing for them to make sure the stone was just right. There are very few who would go to such lengths, modelling for their own memorial stone."

Walsingham was stunned. She wasn't simply a genius,

14

she was a devious, witty and potentially evil one too. If ghosts were able to turn bright red, he knew that was what colour Donne's face would be turning, as his wife delivered her unrelenting assessment. After all, what other man did they know, who had posed for his own tomb? It didn't need emphasising further, he thought, gently squeezing her arm with his, their subtle sign from down the years that a conversation was over, and that they should both move on. It had never failed them, and it didn't now.

"Anyway, Francis, I was just having the sweetest conversation with Anne of Cleves, from the Westminster party, and she was telling me about some of the trouble they've been having, between Elizabeth and the two Marys. Some things simply do not change, do they? I'm confident they never will. But I would quite like a rest now; shall we take a stroll?"

"I think that would be wonderful, Ursula. I feel like we've been both cooped up and on display these last few hours. Let us get some time to ourselves, before normality resumes tomorrow." With the briefest of nods towards Donne, he walked away, squeezing his wife's arm even tighter, to show how pleased he was at the points she had made.

Only when they were safely out of earshot did they stop to sit on a low wall, so he could outline his plan.

"And so Gaunt and Tudor are already making their way through the group, letting them know about the meeting, and so we will see how it all goes."

"I'm sure it will go wonderfully, my dear. But that's tomorrow's concern. For now, I don't think I want to be in St Paul's at all. I would prefer to take a walk along the riverside and get away from all this bustle."

Walsingham nodded, and they made their way slowly to the bank of the Thames. Ursula was right; despite his role at the heart of court during life, now, in death, he was much more in favour of a quiet, calm existence, settled, and knowing where he belonged. And where he belonged was St Paul's, even if they had completely rebuilt the place, even if

15

his tomb had been lost, even if their little community changed beyond recognition.

"I suppose, if you think about it," he said, not giving Ursula chance to catch up with where his thoughts had taken him, "we were always going to have new people coming in, weren't we?"

She blinked at him, twice, before working out where he had got to in his mind. "That's true enough. A cathedral is a cathedral, and until the fire, there's no reason to think we wouldn't have plenty more people buried amongst us."

"In which case, apart from the physical bricks and stone of the building, perhaps nothing has actually changed?" Walsingham mused.

"You could say that."

"And we are actually in a position of strength, rather than weakness, being original residents, rather than newcomers. Of course, we won't have tombs, or markers, but it is our spiritual home, literally, and we have every right to stay here." Walsingham could hear the confidence in his voice growing as his thoughts solidified.

"Quite. Furthermore, we have the backing of Queen Elizabeth, which certainly won't hurt."

She was right. Having the backing of such a well-respected monarch would be of benefit to all of them; such an unforgettable queen still held sway in people's minds. "It won't indeed. But, as you say, this is tomorrow's concern. Come, let's enjoy the rest of our day."

The next morning, hiding from the rest of the ghosts, cloaked in invisibility, and staying hidden behind the quire screen for good measure, Walsingham was hoping he could hide his anxiety as well as he could hide himself. To his delight, in the quarter of an hour before ten o'clock, the spirits of Old St Paul's began to drift into the quire, talking quietly in little groups, one or two standing alone, watching over proceedings, as though unsure exactly why they had been summoned. He was impressed that even the kings had arrived. As he heard a clock chime the hour, he emerged from the shadows. They were well away from the day's construction works, and there was no risk of them being disturbed.

"Your Graces, my Lords, Ladies, and gentlemen," he said, casting his eye around the gathered group. "Thank you for accepting our invitation to join us this morning. As you will be aware, these are interesting times. A number of our little community have already chosen to leave us, and I know that there is uncertainty amongst the rest of you as to what will become of us when the cathedral is finished, and new burials begin to be held here."

There was a murmuring in the group, accompanied by nodding heads, and whispered concerns. Walsingham held up his arms to quieten them.

"Friends, we have been blind in our worries, and yesterday, thankfully, the cloth has been removed from my eyes. We," he gestured to Gaunt and Tudor, "have a solution, and we hope that we have come to an arrangement which will suit everyone."

He paused for effect, waiting until he was sure he had everyone's attention.

"We stay."

"But, can we do that?" The question came from John Howson, the Bishop of Durham in life, but it was clear that he was simply voicing the thoughts of the entire crowd.

Walsingham nodded, then continued. "Why could we not do it? This is our home, whether it has been for a couple of decades, a century, or many centuries. We witnessed its destruction, we have witnessed this start of its rebirth, and we shall witness its final completion. We should not feel as if we are losing our home; we should feel that our home is rising, phoenix-like, from the ashes of this great city. We belong here, and there is no reason, none whatsoever, for us to be concerned about leaving our place of peace. So I say we stay. We watch these walls grow around us, find a new place within them, and when our new neighbours begin to arrive, we shall be here to greet them, in friendship, not anxiety. St Paul's is ours. It shall remain so."

17

The group in front of him was silent. It was to his great relief that he had remembered every word of his carefully-prepared speech, and he was thankful to Ursula for letting him rehearse it at least six times that morning. Then, to his delight, one by one, the nodding which had been done in agreement to their anxiety began again. He felt his own anxiety lessening.

Finally, Robert Morton, another former bishop, this time Bishop of Worcester, rose from his seat. "It would seem, Walsingham, that you have our agreement. We have all been worrying individually on this, I believe, and if we can come together, as one, then there is no reason why your plan should not work out perfectly. If you will indulge my historical knowledge for a moment, I believe it could easily be another decade before we have anyone new joining us, so there is plenty of time for us to make our mark on our new, old, home."

"You are right, Morton," John of Gaunt rose to stand beside Walsingham. "Great churches like these do not rise up overnight. I mean, even to get this far has taken years. I am entirely supportive of this plan, and emphasise the point that if we stand together, it shall remain our home."

More nodding made its way around the group, and still more agreement. This was it; they had the group's agreement. Only Donne did not look impressed. Walsingham smirked to himself. One disgruntled poet was not going to ruin his day. He had saved his little community, and that was that. Whatever the future might throw at them, their collective past would surely be sufficient to hold them together now.

March, 1723

As the spirits gathered in the great space of the cathedral, completed for almost a decade, Walsingham looked around, knowing that back in 1697 they had made the right decision to stay. Their prediction that it would be years before the first burial had been correct; the day had only just arrived, and with it, the expectation of a new ghost joining their little community. They were a strangely happy group. Not as many of the celebrated dead that Westminster Abbey held within its walls, or the infamous terror of the Tower of London, but the spirits that remained had formed fast friendships. And today, they would welcome their newest member.

Strange then, that this new entrant was, in a way, one of the men responsible for all the upheaval, all those years ago: Sir Christopher Wren himself.

The architect was being commemorated that day with a service, and a comparatively simple burial in the eastern end of the crypt. Nothing had been confirmed as to what his final tomb would look like, but bets had been made that some sort of witty statement would be made. Being buried in one's own cathedral wasn't an everyday occurrence, after all.

"So," John of Gaunt's voice pulled Walsingham from his thoughts. "Is everyone content with the day's plan? We shall have no haunting of any variety during the funeral service, and if Sir Christopher does indeed make an appearance, then we stick to the plan that's been in place since opening."

The two Bishops, of Durham and Worcester, rose to their feet in unison, Robert Morton speaking for them both. "We shall be ready at the entrance to the crypt, watching for his spirit, and making it clear, if he does indeed appear, that he is entirely welcome."

"I do hope he doesn't find it impertinent," said Blanche, seated next to Ursula at the front of the group. "I mean, it is sort of 'his' cathedral, after all. Does it not feel a little like welcoming somebody into their own home?"

"I'll confess to a hint of unease about it being Sir Christopher," conceded Walsingham. "But, we did agree that this was our plan. Granted, a noble or monarch would have been easier, but perhaps, in a way, this could work to our advantage. After all, if we welcome Sir Christopher, and he joins our community, choosing to stay with us, then those who follow him into, as you say, his cathedral, then doesn't that mean they will also feel inclined to respect our places here?"

"From what we saw of him during the design and construction process, I don't think we have anything to worry about. After all, if you had built something this grand, and got to be buried within it, wouldn't you want to stay and hear what people had to say about it for years, decades, even centuries to come? I know I would." Ursula smiled at him as she finished speaking. "Having said that, gentlemen," she turned to the Bishops, "perhaps you need to consider your tone. Rather than welcoming him in a 'welcome to our community' sort of way, perhaps phrase it more 'we are pleased to welcome you, and isn't this a wonderful home you built for us all?', if you can see the difference?"

Walsingham could indeed see the difference. They needed to tread carefully, not wishing to alienate their home's architect. Happily the Bishop of Durham was nodding slowly, clearly deep in thought.

"It must feel as though we are glad to have him here, amongst us, and hope that he remains so, and that we simply happen to live here," the Bishop stated. "One must hope he won't be insufferable. We can handle that, I dare say."

A clock chimed, telling them things were about to begin.

***

As the last mourner made their way out of the great doors, Sir Christopher found himself alone in the crypt. He could hear the voices of the two ghosts at the entrance to the space, but wasn't yet ready to be greeted. They would be friendly enough, he hoped – but then, he had been party to the full destruction of their home, and the design of this new one; would that make him some sort of enemy to them?

He could wait no longer. He had met the great and good of society in life; he could certainly do so in death. Summoning his courage, he flashed into visibility, allowing other spirits to see him, and made his way towards their hushed conversation.

"My lords," he greeted them, on seeing their Bishop's robes.

"Sir Christopher," the first stepped forward. "I am Robert Morton, Bishop of Worcester, and it is an honour to meet you."

"Likewise, Sir," the second nodded, a smile on his face. "John Howson, Bishop of Durham. Would you like to meet others of our little band, or do you have other plans?"

"Plans?" Plans hadn't come into it, thought Sir Christopher. Did the dead have plans? "I had assumed we stay with our bodies. Is that not the case? And, Bishops, are you content with this as an afterlife?"

The two men shared an uneasy look, then glanced behind them. Following an almost imperceptible nod from Howson, a third man emerged into the group.

"Sir Christopher, it is an honour. Francis Walsingham, a pleasure to meet you." The man bowed in greeting, which Sir Christopher returned.

"Walsingham? The spymaster?"

"The very same, Sir. Although I assure you, those days are well behind me now."

Sir Christopher didn't believe that for a moment.

Walsingham continued. "I understand you will have many questions, but the first, and main, is that we do indeed have the power to move as we wish, within limits. You certainly do not have to remain here with your body, but we would be extremely honoured if you decided to do so. We are a merry, if rather calm, group, and it is always a pleasure to have new members join us, to share their news, knowledge, and thoughts."

Sir Christopher realised they were waiting for a response. "I suppose it would be interesting, potentially pleasant even, to remain in my own creation. You know, this is going to be a place of such worship, celebration, remembrance, over the years, I am sure of it."

The Bishop of Worcester smiled. "And it would be a shame if the man who gave it to the world wasn't able to enjoy his success, and see and hear people's emotions when

21

they visit. You should meet our ancient kings. There could be centuries of enjoyment ahead of you here."

He had to admit he was tempted. And his was a family tomb, after all. He wouldn't be alone – well, he wouldn't anyway, with so many ghosts clearly already in attendance – but there was a difference between the ghosts of strangers, and the chance of seeing his beloved family as they too were interred within the vault beneath his feet.

He must have nodded, even without fully intending to, based on the expressions which appeared on the faces of the three men in front of him.

"Is that a 'yes' then?" asked Walsingham.

Sir Christopher nodded for certain that time. "It is a 'yes', I believe."

"Excellent, Sir, excellent. Now, come this way. Let me introduce you to those who live in this house you built, and explain exactly how this works…"

Present Day

As the last visitors of the day began making their way to the exits, Sir Christopher found himself standing beside his final resting place. It wasn't as though he frequented it overly, but it gave him some pleasure when people noticed it, and noticed him, even when there were so many more famous than him remembered in the walls of his 'new' cathedral. Aware of movement behind him, he turned, to find Walsingham, Gaunt and Tudor watching him.

"There's talk of a social gathering over the river this evening, meeting at the Globe. Rumours of Shakespeare actually performing, but you never know with these things; rumours start so easily," said Walsingham, gesturing with his head towards the door. "Care to join us?"

Nodding, Sir Christopher followed them, pausing briefly to glance back at the simple inscription above his tomb:

LECTOR, SI MONUMENTUM REQUIRIS, CIRCUMSPICE.

Reader, if you seek his memorial, look around you.

Kindred Spirits: Jailbreak

A version of this story originally appeared on the Discovering Diamonds *blog in December 2018, in response to their call-out to write a piece of historical fiction inspired by a song.*

"Right then, if there's nothing else to discuss, I think that brings our meeting to a close." Richard III clapped his hands together, making a few of the more distracted ghosts jump, and causing poor Margaret Pole to fall off the edge of the pew she had been perching on.

"Not mentioning it doesn't mean it won't happen, brother." The Duke of Clarence rose from his place, winking at Anne Boleyn as he did so. "The ten-yearly meeting of The Escapees is due this weekend, as well you know."

There was a general murmur throughout the group, as memories of previous years, and their associated chaos, was remembered.

Richard sighed. "Yes, alright. Nothing special lined up this year, as far as I know, just please everyone, be aware we'll be seeing a few different faces around." There was a collective nod from the group gathered in front of him, in the chapel at the heart of the White Tower for their weekly meeting, before their usual more relaxed nightly gathering. He hoped this year would go smoothly; hardly any of the previous visits had. Not that he could put his finger on it, but something about their rebellious nature perhaps? It was an elite club, after all: those who had successfully escaped the most notorious prison in the land...

The 5th of September started badly for Richard. Before he could threaten his brother with unspeakable punishment for doing so, Clarence woke him with deliberately tuneless singing.

"But it makes no sense!" Richard cried, as George Boleyn joined in for the second verse. "Where else would a jailbreak be in a town, other than at the jail? It's ridiculous!" If he ever met a member of Thin Lizzy, he was going to have to have strong words with them; a jailbreak was hardly going to be in the library or shopping centre, was it?

The two Georges were having none of it, celebrating the day, every decade, when members of that infamous group, the Escapees, returned to the Tower, celebrating their great escapes on the death-date of their first member, Ranulf Flambard. The day never passed quietly. After two further renditions, the trio met Katherine Howard and Anne Boleyn at the main gate, to greet their guests.

"Friends, welcome," said Richard.

Roger Mortimer stepped forward, before Flambard demanded priority over the alleged murderer of Edward II.

"Ladies first, surely," came the thoughtful voice of the Earl of Nithsdale, urging his wife forward.

Richard turned to the Georges. "Keep an eye on things. I want the re-enactments, a couple of minor hauntings, then they can join the gathering this evening. Nothing more, understood?"

To Richard's relief, the group had apparently decided that this was the year they were going to listen to him. Almost. The gasps of shock in the old animal house were fine, and more than acceptable, but the glimpse of a medieval lord flickering just outside the chapel earned Mortimer a strict reprimand from Jane Grey. In the end, Mortimer resorted to using George Clarence's usual trick of loitering near the infamous re-creation of the barrel he was executed in, and giving Clarence a break from haunting.

There was always something satisfying about an easy haunt, thought Richard, as he wandered around the Tower, greeting the occasional ghost he encountered, and staying out of the way of the living. Whilst they had guests visiting, and being keen to make an impression during their time, most of the resident ghosts kept themselves to themselves. Apart from the regulars, not many were out and about until their evening meeting on the top floor of the White Tower.

That was the point where things became more entertaining. With tourists gone for the day, and the living residents of the Tower safely tucked up in their homes for the night, or relaxing in their private pub, the White Tower became entirely the domain of the dead. Now was the time for gossip to be shared, stories to be told, and laughter to be enjoyed throughout the group. There were no restrictions on a party when it created no disturbance, after all.

It was gone midnight before the party finally ended, with everyone, residents and visitors alike, settling down and hoping for a quiet night after an eventful day and evening.

They wouldn't get their wish.

"Richard!" The hissed voice woke him.

"Who's there? What time is it? What's up?"

"Anne, gone three, and we have a problem."

Appearing through his door, Richard began to ask questions, but Anne was already walking away, explaining as she went.

"There's a girl stuck outside. A Beefeater's daughter, not supposed to be out, faked being in bed with pillows, and managed to fall out with whoever's party it was."

A group of ghosts had gathered: the Georges, Jane Grey, Katherine Howard, and the Escapees. Richard looked around, talking through the situation. "So, the doors are all locked from the inside, she's not meant to be out there, and if she knocks, she'll be in all sorts of trouble."

"So, brother, what do we do?" asked Clarence.

The Nithsdales shared a look of unhidden glee. "We help her."

Richard saw their train of thought unfolding. "Oh no. If you're thinking what I think you're thinking, no."

The Earl grinned. "But it's perfect. Tonight of all nights."

"Or, we put one of the guards on watch, make sure no harm comes to her, and let her find her own way in when the doors open again in the morning," said Richard, trying to beat the tide he was sure was going to overthrow him.

"Oh yes, I see where this is going!" said Boleyn, grabbing his sister and twirling her around in a manic dance.

Richard knew he was beaten. "Fine. But if we do this, if we help her break in, we do this my way. And we do it sensibly."

Anne Boleyn extricated herself from her brother's arms as Richard outlined his plan. No names, no titles, give the quickest, most efficient help they could offer, then move on as though the whole thing had never happened.

"Oh, come now, Richard – it has to be more fun than that. Katherine and I shall go and find her house, get a spare key somehow, whilst you," she pointed at the Georges and Richard, "must get the key to the outer gate, and distract the guards sufficiently to get her inside."

"You make it sound so easy," the Plantagenet king scoffed. "Oh, alright, let's get to it. I'll go and see the girl. Will you join me?" He looked at Jane, who nodded. "And you all, please, help with some gentle distraction?"

The Escapees grinned, beginning to look for inspiration as the rest of the ghostly group went about their assigned tasks.

At the waterfront, Richard and Jane approached the girl. "Are you alright?" he asked softly, gently flickering into full visibility, hoping she wouldn't bolt.

The girl looked up, eyes wide, evidently about to scream, then, nothing.

"Please, don't be afraid," said Jane, joining Richard. "We are here to help, we promise. We, well, we overheard your predicament."

"But, but, no." The girl rubbed at her eyes, as though trying to erase the vision. Then she moved as it to flee, grabbing her bag and jumping from the bench.

26

"Please!" Jane reached for the girl's arm, halting her. "We won't hurt you."

"What's your name?" asked Richard.

"Cl... Claire. You're... ghosts?"

"Well, yes, but we see you're in trouble, and we're all neighbours really, and we want to help."

"My parents don't know I'm out; they said I couldn't go," Claire whispered, as though not quite believing what she was doing. "I'm stuck."

"We have that in hand," said Richard, glancing over at the thick wooden door, hoping he was right. As he watched, his brother's head appeared through the wood, accompanied by a hand, giving a thumbs-up. They were on.

"Claire, if you trust us, we can help you. Right now, what other options do you really have?"

She hesitated. "I don't want to wake up tomorrow thinking I'm mad and dreamed it all."

Richard nodded. "If you come with us now, and we get you in, tomorrow we'll introduce to some of our more famous contingent. But please, move?"

A cry from within the walls distracted them, and Richard flitted through to see what distraction the Escapees had gone for. He couldn't help laughing, as the Nithsdales were performing a perfect waltz in full view, the two guards on duty standing gaping. Boleyn slipped between them, removing the keys from the small room they guarded. A moment later, the door, luckily well-oiled, swung open, and Jane ushered Claire through.

But it wasn't over yet. The two guards weren't the only ones about, and Claire still needed to get home. She stayed in darkness, hugging the walls, as she crept towards the row of houses leading down from St Peter's. Suddenly, light flooded the area. Torchlight, sweeping in an arc across the Jewel House. A Beefeater, out of bed, and a major risk to their plan.

Richard took his chance.

"Beware this night," he whispered into the man's ear, adding a hint of ghostly moan. "You should not walk this

27

night, it shall not be safe for those who do…" Richard cringed at his own melodramatic approach, but he had to scare the man back inside somehow. It didn't seem to faze him, as he kept shining his torch. Katherine Howard timed her entrance – head under arm, lips moving in silence – to perfection. If a ghostly moan wouldn't deter him, a headless woman certainly did, as the torch was dropped, lens shattering.

"I'd forgotten how much fun a decent headless haunt can be," said Katherine, giggling, as she spotted Claire, standing open-mouthed at the sight. "Go on – Anne has a key ready for you at your door," the former queen continued.

"Anne? Not, Boleyn?"

"Yes, who else?" asked Katherine.

"Please, Claire, go. Who knows who else is about?" said Richard, in full visibility, physically grabbing her shoulders and moving towards her home, thankfully still in darkness.

"I'll see you tomorrow? Promise?"

"Yes, I promise. We'll be about; we always are."

Frowning, she turned the retrieved key in her lock, and pushed the door. In silence, she was inside, the door reclosed, and the lock clicked back into place.

"Are we really going to find her tomorrow?" asked Anne. All the dead were now invisible to the living.

"I have no idea," confessed Richard. "We did promise, I suppose. Tomorrow isn't that far away now, so we don't have long to decide. Come on, let's see if anyone's still about."

In the White Tower's chapel, a few ghosts were loitering, keen to hear what had been unfolding.

"Is it true then?" demanded Margaret Pole. "Are we to make ourselves visible for that young thing? What if she tells everyone else? What if we just become another tourist attraction?"

"We already are a tourist attraction, my dear," said Clarence, patting his daughter's hand. "But I do see your point. When they don't *know* we're here, we keep our mystery. Now she does, who knows where it will lead? She could even go to the papers."

"But who would believe her?" Anne Boleyn walked through the door, literally, into the discussion. "Besides, how would that help her? She would have to admit she'd been out. No, we're safe. If she tells what happened, she brings a heap of trouble down on herself. I've seen her around, and I don't think she's the type to want that. However, in terms of tomorrow…" She glanced around the small group, including the visiting Escapees. "… I suggest we limit things. I say we don't add more than one or two others to those she's met so far. Keep it simple."

"Agreed," said George Boleyn. "It could be quite good fun, this, having an 'inside man'." He glanced over at Clarence, grins spreading across their faces.

Anne smiled at Richard, and nodded. "I think we might have an interesting time ahead."

Kindred Spirits:
Carlisle Castle

It had begun peacefully, just like every year. Then, again, just like every year, things had got out of hand.

"After all these years, decades, centuries even, you'd think this could be better handled by now?" mused Queen Mary to the young soldier standing beside her, as they looked down on the proceedings.

William hadn't been picked for the Carlisle Castle team, and had instead chosen to stay on the castle walls with his former prisoner, who, luckily for him, had deemed him unworthy of having a grudge held against him. He nodded to the Scots Queen, as he and his colleagues had called her when they were watching her, centuries before. "I'd like to say the Jacobites team start it each year, Madame, but sadly, I think this year our guards are as much to blame."

It had started with a foul, potentially in what had been roughly designated the Castle Guards' penalty area thanks to some stolen jumpers and cones. But, ghosts being ghosts, one or two had been spirited forward before the referee (an old guardsman from the cathedral) had wheezed his way up the pitch to sort things out. He hadn't made it in time, and in less than a minute both teams were engaged in what would have been a fight to the death, if they weren't already dead.

"I suppose, in one way, it's safer now there cannot be too many actual injuries," Queen Mary said. Suddenly, her attention was drawn to a commotion at the other end of the field. If she had still had a heart, it would have pushed harder inside her chest at the sight. A group of locals, very drunk by the look (and sound) of them, were heading haphazardly towards the makeshift pitch. "Oh, here we go."

She signalled to William, and the pair floated from the battlements to the ground below.

The teams had heard the approaching gang, and frozen, invisible to the living, watching as they tried to work out what the newcomers would do.

Seeing the pitch set up, in the middle of the night, the locals paused for a moment, wondering aloud whether they had disrupted an ongoing match, or found the remnants of one long finished. Little did they know, the battle they had disturbed had been ongoing for longer than anyone living could remember.

"Well?" One of the local lads had reached the football. "What do you reckon?" He looked around his group of friends, clearly trying to count through the alcohol-induced fog.

"We're one short for five-a-side, mate." His friend had been quicker at the maths. "But since Smithy's played for the town, he counts as two, so his side only needs four men." Laughing, the second man ducked as the aforementioned Smithy found a discarded baseball cap and sent it spinning through the air at his friend.

"Let's go short sleeves versus long," called another of the group.

As they looked around, they evidently realised it would work. A general murmur of agreement spread around the men, and they formed themselves, staggeringly, into the two agreed teams.

The Jacobites and the Guards had barely moved during the whole interlude. Now, meeting each other's eyes and realising here was not only a greater danger but also a greater opportunity, they silently broke away, mid-fight. On the sideline, Queen Mary watched on, smiling at what she hoped was about to unfold. There was the odd haunting within the walls of Carlisle Castle, but it didn't have the reputation of some places, once you left the more enclosed areas. And there was nothing wrong with a little fun now and then, was there? Even ghosts needed entertainment.

In a heartbeat, if ghosts had heartbeats, Jacobites and

Guards had found their football stolen, their match abandoned, and a new game about to begin. But even arch-enemies could work together for a common cause. The local lads were drunk enough that the odd glimpse of a ghostly uniformed guard might be missed; the dead might need something stronger.

The referee was finally able to take charge. "There's two teams of them, lads, two teams of us, for five-a-side. It's perfect. I reckon we gives them a run for their money, what do you say?" He didn't even wait for a response before marching onwards, towards the gaggle, now having successfully navigated themselves into formation. The ball had been retrieved and placed as near to the centre-spot as they could manage, with the lads shouting instructions back and forth.

In the centre of the field, the referee raised his fingers to his mouth, and in the quickest flash of visibility, blew hard, his whistle bringing the lads' jostling to a halt.

"What the…?"

"Who was that?"

The rush of panic flooded out of them, as each glanced at the others, hoping to see evidence of one of them having done it. There was nothing. None of them had brought a whistle.

"Bad timing lads, must have been a chimney somewhere, or somebody mucking around over there." Smithy nodded back towards town, but didn't look convinced, even as he spoke.

Luckily, the referee had more wits than the locals, and gestured to one of the Guards, who whistled himself, further off, more quietly. It was enough to settle the lads, who resumed their positions, laughing at their own mistakes.

The castle comrades grinned, glancing at their ref for the go-ahead. A nod was all it took. The game was on.

It was almost unfair. Ten fit men with the ability to hover, control their visibility and move anything unseen, against nine who could hardly walk in a straight line. For the first few minutes, the drunks simply thought themselves more worse for wear than they imagined.

Then came the severed head.

It was about the same dimension as a football, and Mary was happy to take part in the jest. There might as well be some silver-lining to having been decapitated. As long as she didn't let her wretched cousin Elizabeth know...

She timed it beautifully, watching for the exact moment one of the locals kicked the ball, remarkably deftly given the state he was in, curving it around his opponent, up and towards the goal. The keeper reached up, stretching for the ball, only for the ball to turn into a female head, bloodied cords of sinew dangling, eyes wide and staring right into his.

His scream was not dignified, as he collapsed into a heap, as the ball, now once again just a ball, fell at his feet and bounced onwards into the goal.

"Did you see...? "Did you...?" He was too shocked to even finish his sentences. And of course, they hadn't seen a thing. Mary Stuart was a professional haunter, whatever the situation.

"Come on, man, you getting up again or what?"

"Can't handle his pints. Go on, swap over, we'll go four-a-side."

"And then there were eight," Queen Mary said, smiling at the Jacobites and Guards nearest to her. "Is anyone in any rush to get back to the castle? Nothing keeping you?"

"Nothing at all, Your Grace." The referee spoke for them all.

This was one match the castle would win, united.

Kindred Spirits:
The Sisterhood of
Hampton Court Palace

A version of this story originally appeared in the Elementary Sisterhood *anthology of short stories, released in 2018.*

"Do you think they'll turn up?" Anne of Cleves looked out across the open space to the small building where the tickets were sold, despite knowing those she waited for were not constrained by such modern matters. Ghosts do not need to worry about entry fees. Or entrances, for that matter.

Sir Isaac Newton offered her a comforting pat on the arm. "None of them said they would not, so logically, we must assume that they will."

Anne nodded at her friend, the one she had planned this with so carefully: her wish to bring together some of the greatest ladies in Britain's history. She had entrusted the verbal invitations to the most reliable guards from the confines of Westminster Abbey, sending them out with plenty of notice, all told to emphasise the day and date as clearly as they could. All had come back, reporting success in finding their quarry. This had been an achievement in itself, considering it wasn't known how active some of the women she had sought actually were. A scuffle of activity behind them jolted Anne from her thoughts, and made both turn and look back into the courtyard behind them – but it was only children, tussling with wooden swords, each threatening the other with a swift beheading. She was glad some of her expected guests weren't there to hear that...

She looked at the crowds beginning to build for the day. There had been an actor earlier, dressed as her ex-husband, making his way through the corridors, there to re-enact the final of the king's weddings. Even after all this time, the image sent shivers down what would have been her spine, if ghosts had spines. "I just hope he doesn't show up," she muttered to Sir Isaac, knowing the great scientist was intelligent enough to know who she was referring to. "I mean, it is his palace, after all."

"As it was yours, and theirs, My Lady. A key part of each of your lives," he replied. "And besides, there's never been any reports, not even from Windsor. Hopefully we will get full confirmation of that, if Queen Jane does decide to join us."

The former Queen of England nodded. Their idea – to bring together that famous, or infamous, collection of women – formed on a lazy day in Westminster Abbey, was starting to feel very real, and not entirely sensible. It had originally been born out of mild curiosity, but what if all the other five did indeed turn up, and weren't willing to enter into the spirit she had intended? Should she have considered bringing some sort of security, or at least some of the other spirits from the Abbey, in case things got out of hand? Or somebody quick-witted, to lighten the mood?

The appearance of two women in Tudor finery broke her train of thought. For a moment, she passed them off as more costumed re-enactors, then she recognised the face of the younger woman. In truth, she was barely more than a girl.

"Katherine!" Anne opened her arms as the girl's face broke into a smile, and her feet into a run.

"Your Grace, um, Anne, um, hello!" Katherine Howard stumbled through her greeting to the older woman, but the embrace the women shared was genuine.

As they broke apart, Katherine turned to her companion. "May I introduce you? Anne, meet Anne!" She burst into giggles. "This is the strangest introduction. Queen Anne Boleyn, please meet Queen Anne of Cleves. I do hope you will get along."

"I personally see no reason why we should not, my dear," said Anne of Cleves, curtseying gracefully to the third woman.

Anne Boleyn responded in kind, mirroring the depth and duration of the honour. "And neither do I, Your Grace. I know you were a good friend to my cousin, and besides, you and I never 'clashed' as it were. But there are others here I am less keen to be reunited with."

Instinctively, all three looked around, but unless invisible, they were the only ghosts present.

"I should ask after my daughter," said Anne Boleyn, turning to her new acquaintance.

"Elizabeth is… well," Anne of Cleves replied carefully. "We still have the occasional bout of activity in that department. She and her sister, sorry, half-sister… I'm sure you understand? Even since the thawing of relations between them, I'd say life is calmer for the whole community when they are apart."

Anne Boleyn laughed gently. "Like mothers, like daughters. Well, enough of her. She has done little enough for me, in life or death. And now we are here," she cast her hands about her, "we should take the chance to explore. And Katherine, my pet, you shall have your chance to be your own ghost, running along your famous corridor, racing to Henry in the hope of being saved." They all knew the tale of Katherine's reputed ghost, still haunting the palace. Or not, as it happened.

Katherine shivered. "It was not a happy time," she said.

Anne of Cleves nodded and put her arm around Katherine's shoulders. News of the poor young queen's arrest, her shock and terror, and confusion, had spread through London faster than anything that had ever been said about herself. Even if she couldn't have run along the corridor as it was claimed she had, the emotions attributed to her spirit were real enough. "Have you never visited?"

"Never," Katherine confirmed. "I arrived at the Tower, after, well, the block, met up with Anne and the others, and decided that there was little point in returning, even on visits. What good could it do? Besides, I was waiting for Thomas." She smiled slightly at her mention of her lover's name. "I never needed to come exploring."

"We at the Tower don't often go exploring too far beyond our walls," said Anne Boleyn. "We have plenty going on as it is, with one thing or another. A few day-trips for some of our residents, but nothing too long-term."

Anne of Cleves didn't doubt it. Legends of the Tower of London and its hauntings were spread far and wide. She had visited the place as an honoured Queen of England – thankfully, never as a prisoner, although she knew she had come close as Henry VIII had started to turn away from her. Her role as Henry's 'beloved sister' had been a strange path to tread for all those years following their annulment, but at least she had had a path to tread, and hadn't fallen victim to the block like so many others during the reigns of the Tudor clan.

"Well, I have no notion as to when the others will be arriving, so I wondered, shall we just make our way in?" Anne of Cleves gestured into the large Base Court. "I know we all lived here at one time or other, but having had a brief wander around earlier, I see much has changed."

"I hear the room I gave birth in is now an office." A small, shy voice made them all turn.

Anne Boleyn was first to speak, through gritted teeth. "Jane. You came."

Jane Seymour nodded gracefully to Anne of Cleves before replying. "I did. I was happy to receive the invitation." She smiled at Katherine, before turning back to Anne Boleyn. "It has been a long time, Anne."

"A long time since you stole my husband, took my throne, and helped usher me to the block? Yes, yes I suppose it has been." There was a shake to her voice, even though she obviously tried to contain it; this was clearly a line she had been rehearsing.

"Come, now, ladies. This is to be a peaceful day." Anne of Cleves gently manœuvred herself to stand almost between the two women, who were now standing face to face.

"I would not have chosen for you to die," Jane said, quietly, but looking Anne Boleyn straight in the eye. "And it is not as though I held your place for very long, is it?"

Anne Boleyn did not respond. Instead, she looked at Anne of Cleves. "You were saying? We shall take a walking tour whilst we await the others' arrival." Without waiting, she marched off.

Katherine placed a hand on Anne of Cleves's arm. "I think she is nervous about seeing Katherine of Aragon, though she will never admit it," she whispered to the remaining women.

"Well, if the great Anne Boleyn feels even half of the guilt I feel on seeing her, then it is understandable," said Jane. She turned to them both. "I did not 'help usher her to the block' as she claims. You know how it was. None of us women had a choice in which direction we were sent, did we? However much she claims she chose her own path. Women did not have their own paths. Not even queens."

Anne and Katherine shook their heads.

"I think," said Anne of Cleves, "on reflection, we might all have chosen differently, if it had been in our hands to do so."

"Are you ladies coming, or are you going to stand there and chatter all day?" Anne Boleyn's voice cut through the air.

Without another word, the three queens followed her, and slipped through the brick walls into the palace itself.

Unseen, Catherine Parr watched them enter, before silently following on behind. It was going to be a strange day, she could tell, but, she hoped, a positive one, once these arguments were over and done with.

"You forget just how big this place is, don't you?" said Katherine to the rest of the group. "When I first came to court, I used to get hopelessly lost, and was always having to ask people to help me. I felt such a fool."

"I was the same – and with hardly any English, it was even harder for me," said Anne of Cleves, as they entered the Great Hall.

"It is funny, I suppose, to think that each of us has presided over feasts, dances and masques within these walls. It played its part for us all," said Anne Boleyn. She looked up at the carved eavesdroppers, and the huge tapestries which lined the walls.

Suddenly, Katherine spotted Catherine Parr enter from under the wooden panelled arches. "And now we are five!"

"Your Graces." The newcomer dipped into a gracious curtsey, which all returned. "It is strange, I think, that our names are so intertwined as part of a group, and yet, some of us have never met, in life or death."

Katherine Howard did the honours of introductions, as each woman greeted Catherine in turn. She and Anne of Cleves had been aware of Lady Latimer (as she had been known at court before her marriage to Henry), but it was still a strange meeting.

"How was he, at the very end?" Jane asked of her, once they had greeted each other.

"Difficult. You will have seen him, I am sure, and the smell…" Catherine's voice trailed away. "I imagine it was also as bad for you?" She turned to Katherine Howard and Anne of Cleves. They nodded.

"He was so handsome in his youth," mused Anne Boleyn. She turned to Jane and spoke directly to her for the first time since leaving the courtyard. "I suppose, for all our disagreements, you, Katherine of Aragon and I at least had him in his prime, a true prince amongst men, and not the monster he became."

"To watch him joust was an awe-inspiring spectacle," said Jane. "The pounding of the hooves, all the colour and show, the music and cheering."

"Until his accident," said Anne Boleyn.

"Until his accident," agreed Jane.

All five women nodded. They knew all about his terrible riding accident, when he had been briefly unconscious, and certainly never the same since. The damage, to his mind as well as his body, had had repercussions for the whole court, but especially for his wives.

"I have to ask, Jane: has he ever appeared?" Katherine Howard looked at the one who shared his grave.

"I was there, for the funeral, as I know you were," Jane replied, looking to Catherine Parr, who nodded in response. "I waited inside what was to be our joint tomb for days, wanting to be there to welcome him, hardly daring to breathe, and certainly not daring to move, in case he arrived and was angry to find I was not there and waiting for him," she continued, as the others hung on her every word.

"Well?"

"He never came. A week or more, it must have been. I didn't move. Didn't speak to anyone. Edward IV was so kind; he kept trying to encourage me to rest, saying that he would keep watch. Elizabeth Woodville too. As Henry's grandmother, she was so caring, and I think she hoped to see him too. But I couldn't leave. Eventually, I must have lost focus, or nodded off, because when I came to, I had been moved into one of the side-chapels, out of the way, and they watched me like hawks to stop me going back down there for a good few weeks."

"At least you had somebody to look out for you," said Anne of Cleves. "It was a strange time, once he had left us. Strange indeed."

"But he definitely hasn't appeared?" asked Katherine Howard again, keen to confirm one way or the other. They were all aware of the importance of a spirit passing through the fabled white light, and how, once entered, there was no way back, not that anyone knew of. If Henry had gone, he was gone.

"If he did stay around as a ghost, I'd like to think he would have come to see at least one or two of us, either dead or alive," said Catherine Parr. "Then again, he cannot have come to see me, or I'm sure my poor Thomas would have been subjected to a haunting or two."

"Have you seen your Thomas?" asked Anne of Cleves.

41

"I think the shame of the treason charge was too much for him," mused Catherine. "He certainly never came visiting after his death."

"But he," Katherine Howard started, before being elbowed in the ribs by Anne Boleyn and shocked into silence.

"I am sure you are right; he was a proud man, from what I recall of him," Anne Boleyn said, looking directly at Catherine Parr. "Come, shall we continue?" She steered her cousin in front of her, and made her way through to the Watching Chamber, behind the Great Hall itself.

"What was that about?" hissed Katherine Howard. "We saw Thomas and his brother only yesterday, however much you pretend otherwise."

"Think, Cousin. If Catherine hears Tom Seymour is present, and in the Tower, how do you think she will feel, knowing that he is choosing to spend eternity with us instead of her? And not even having visited his poor sister Jane, alone and miserable in Windsor?"

Katherine's shoulders sagged. "Of course. Oh, how stupid of me. So, we say nothing about the Seymour brothers?"

Anne Boleyn nodded. "That's right. Not one word. About either of them. It won't help anyone."

Katherine nodded, as the group continued their tour.

Whilst the other women were otherwise engaged, the first of their number, Queen Katherine of Aragon, was the last to arrive. Even as she sauntered, unseen to the living, past the groups of tourists, and into the great open space of Base Court, she wasn't convinced she had made the right decision. She had been Queen of England when this palace first came into prominence; she had been a loved, loving and loyal wife and consort, yet had still managed to end her days alone, and abandoned by the man most associated with this building. Most people didn't even realise Katherine had held that seemingly prized position for so long: over twenty years, far longer than the other, practically flash-in-the-pan wives and queens who had followed her. She hadn't needed to come. And yet here she was.

As though from nowhere, the ghost of a man appeared before her, sweeping a low, respectful bow, showing full deference. She nodded to him in return, curious as to who had been sent to meet her.

"My Lady, Your Grace, Queen Katherine; it is an honour to be here to greet you. I am Sir Isaac Newton, and I am here to advise you that the others are all here, and making their way through the palace."

"I am not late?"

"No, of course not, there was never any time agreed, after all. They merely thought they would take a stroll, until you were able to join them. Would you like me to go on ahead and locate them, to save you the inconvenience of having to find them yourself?"

Katherine nodded. Without intending to, her eyes flicked across the front of the building. So, Anne Boleyn was in here somewhere. The knowledge that her rival and successor could potentially be looking out through any of these windows filled her with unease. I should be stronger than this, she thought, pulling herself up to her full height, what little there was of it compared to some of the others. "I shall make my way to the so-called haunted corridor, then down to the kitchens. I have no need to see the exhibition concerning my own time here." She had done her homework, and knew about the exhibition of 'Young Henry' and the tangled relationship between him, Cardinal Wolsey (the first owner of the property) and herself.

"Very good, Your Grace." With another low bow, Sir Isaac hurried away.

Looking around her, then choosing to do things the old-fashioned way, Katherine made her way along the same path the others had followed so soon before, across the court and up the short flight of stairs to the Great Hall, watching Sir Isaac rush on ahead of her.

A scream alerted her to the probable location of the group, in the famous haunted corridor. Katherine of Aragon decided to go straight to the kitchens instead, and prepare for their arrival.

"Something touched me, I swear it!" The woman was staring about wildly, as the five former Queens of England tried desperately to stifle their giggles and act like the royal women they were.

"Don't be stupid, there's nothing here. Nobody's anywhere near you." The lady's friend scolded her, although her wide eyes belied her confidence.

"It must have been Katherine Howard," the little boy with them piped up, his face alight with the idea of a real ghost actually haunting his group. "I want her to haunt me too!"

"No you do not. It's not a ghost, it must have just been a draught," the second woman told him. "Come on, let's keep moving. Don't cause a commotion." She stared pointedly at her friend, who was now trying to pull herself together.

It had indeed been Katherine Howard, and she wasn't finished yet. "If he wants to be haunted, who are we to disappoint?" she said, stepping forward and blowing gently in his ear.

The small boy had apparently been lying. On being haunted himself, it all proved too much, and he started crying, rushing to his mother and grabbing at her legs. "Mummy, I got haunted! I don't like it! I want to go!"

Katherine Howard froze, the giggles of her co-haunters suddenly stifled. "Too much?" she mouthed. Her cousin Anne Boleyn nodded in response.

Catherine Parr took charge. "Come on. Let's make our way to the kitchens; it is less controversial, and a small bit of light haunting will not cause any harm there, I am sure."

"An excellent idea, Your Grace." Sir Isaac joined them, having been watching from a distance. "Her Grace Katherine of Aragon is here, and, I believe, shall be shortly making her own way to the kitchens and hoping to await you there."

The women all noticed Anne Boleyn's back straighten at

the name of the Spanish princess. This was going to get interesting. Katherine Howard tried her best to delay the inevitable. "Perhaps we should go via those offices Jane mentioned earlier? I'm sure I saw one of those nice ladies from television earlier, the curators?"

"Which one?" Anne of Cleves asked.

"The one with the blonde bob. I've seen her in programmes; she always seems to wear such nice dresses," Katherine replied.

"From what I've seen, her wardrobe is truly envy-inspiring," said Anne of Cleves.

"Oh, come on, will you?" Anne Boleyn said, irritation clear in her voice. "Let's get this over with."

The great fire in the kitchen was ablaze. The heat was getting too much for some of the visitors, who moved on quickly to the rest of the exhibits which today included actors making medieval bread.

"My stomach would be rumbling if it could. That bread smells delicious," said Catherine Parr, trying to defuse the tension she knew was bubbling near the surface. Katherine of Aragon was standing behind the actors, watching their activity intently, yet Catherine had a feeling the older woman knew perfectly well that the five queens had just entered. Here was a woman who had been in European courts practically her whole life, and who was so attuned to every detail. She had dealt with Henry VIII and his play-acting for over twenty years. She was certainly not a woman to miss her greatest rival entering a room.

Jane followed Catherine's lead. "I know. It is so cruel, is it not, that our sense of smell remains, yet we cannot enjoy the taste any more. I found it the hardest thing to deal with on my death."

Anne Boleyn had paused at the entrance to the room, but now pulled herself up to her full height, repositioned her jewels, and stepped forward. None of the other women moved.

"Your Grace," she said, inclining her head, but refraining

from dipping into a curtsey.

Katherine of Aragon looked up. "Anne Boleyn. I had wondered whether we would ever meet again. And here we are, back in Hampton Court, so many centuries later." Her voice was level, composed. "Things didn't quite work out how you hoped, did they?"

Her successor blinked, but did not flinch. Both had clearly prepared for this meeting, the one everyone had surely dreaded the most.

Katherine continued: "You destroyed a queen, caused the fall of a religion, tore a country – almost a continent – in two, and for what? The same twist of fate which plagued me: a single living daughter, dismissal, then death. Was it worth it?" The calm, steady tone of Katherine's voice was more powerful than if she had been screaming, each point striking the blow she intended.

Anne faltered. She opened her mouth to speak, but found nothing. Again she tried; again, silence. Katherine kept her gaze level. Finally, Anne found her voice. "It wasn't my fault. I was fertile, just as you were. It wasn't my fault." She spun round and appealed to the rest of the group. "Well? What say you? Edward might have been a miracle after all, the one Henry prayed for, for all those years, but I'll bet you anything, Jane, that had you lived, there would have been no string of siblings to follow him. And you, Catherine – your own poor little Mary conceived, what, almost immediately on your marriage to Tom Seymour? Yet nothing with Henry. I could have given any other man a handful of heirs, a dynasty of daughters. But not him. None of us could."

"But you found out too late," said Katherine of Aragon, drawing Anne's attention back to herself. "And Elizabeth wasn't enough to keep you your throne, just as Mary wasn't enough for me."

"I could have kept him, if not for the plotting." Anne's voice was starting to break with emotion.

"Yes, it hurts, doesn't it, to be plotted against, rather than plotting yourself?" Katherine's tone was biting.

"You should have retired! You know there was never going to be a Prince of Wales, you could have been a revered woman, practically a saint!"

"Retired? He was my husband. You do not 'retire' from a blessed union. You stay loyal, and you work around any problems which God chooses to send you. In whatever form those problems are shaped. You should have followed your sister's lead. She was the sensible one of you two. Of all three of you Boleyns."

"You dare bring my sister into this? She ended up with nothing!" Anne was almost hoarse.

"Nothing apart from the love of a good, true man, and a life lived happily away from court with her family around her. Yes, nothing indeed. Whilst you had it all, and lived so happily, with no troubles to crease your brow?"

"No! It should have worked. Everything should have worked." Anne's emotions finally got the better of her, and the tears began to fall. Catherine Parr and Katherine Howard rushed to her side, her cousin wrapping her in a tight embrace.

Feeling things start to get out of hand, Anne of Cleves looked across the warring women at Sir Isaac. He nodded in response to her raised eyebrow; it was time to put their plan into action, the plan Anne had conceived in case this situation arose. In truth, she had practised it a dozen times over the past few weeks. It would seem they had all come prepared with something they needed to say to the others.

"Ladies, please! We are all civilised women – we are all former Queens of England, for however long we reigned."

"Says she who had a mere six months. You say we are the same, when I had twenty-four years, more than all of you combined. Doubly so," retorted Katherine of Aragon, her voice raised for the first time since they entered the room. The outburst shocked them all into silence.

"We have all had more than however long we reigned in life," replied Anne of Cleves, stepping forward. "That's why I asked you all here today. It's been happening for a few centuries now. You must have felt it? The change, the shift towards us, and away from Henry?"

A moment of silence.

"They retitled us 'Queen' when they reinterred our bodies," said Katherine Howard, gently easing her cousin away from her hug, and looking her in the eye.

Anne Boleyn nodded, and wiped her eyes, trying to compose herself. "All of the Beefeaters show us nothing but respect these days. And the books, fact or fiction, they see our side of things, more and more." Her voice was broken, but sounded stronger with each word.

"There are always fresh flowers on my grave," conceded Katherine of Aragon. "And sometimes, people bring pomegranates; it's a small gesture, but a kind one."

"Pomegranates?" Katherine Howard looked across, her eyebrows raised.

Katherine of Aragon smiled, a bitterness to her expression. "My personal emblem. There are still a few of them around this place, if you look hard enough; he couldn't fully erase any of us, however hard he tried. It was also a symbol of fertility."

The irony wasn't lost on any of them.

"My grave was beautiful, in the end, despite a few misadventures along the way," added Catherine Parr.

"And I have pride of place, in the heart of Westminster." Anne of Cleves finished the rounding off. Or so she thought.

"I never really get noticed." Jane Seymour's voice was scarcely audible. "They opened my vault up for Henry himself, then Charles I, and then again for a poor child of Queen Anne's in the 1690s, lost even before birth. All those feet, every day; I doubt anyone sees anything more than Henry's name before moving on."

Katherine of Aragon and Anne of Cleves both moved at the same moment, seeing the threat of tears in Jane's eyes. Each took an arm, linking their own through hers.

"You gave him a son," said Anne of Cleves, trying to silently urge the others to join her in her encouragement.

All but Anne Boleyn took the hint, following the other Anne's sentiment.

"He chose you to be buried with, my dear, you should never forget that," said Catherine Parr, above the murmurings. "And you are in the centre of his family portrait. You, at least, are at the heart of things, seeing celebrations all the time, not buried away from everyone and everything, to be disturbed time and time again. I was lost, re-discovered, re-buried... It's been such a mess. And I wasn't even in that family portrait, despite being married to him when he commissioned it."

Jane freed her arms and ran her hands over her face. "We are all, indeed, the heroines and survivors of our own stories, I suppose, even if some of us played a role in the downfall of our predecessor."

Katherine of Aragon and Anne Boleyn studiously looked anywhere but at each other.

"Jane is right," Katherine Howard spoke up. "What is the point in us arguing, and hating one another now, after so long?"

"Better for us to work together, towards a common goal – ensuring our monster of a husband is seen as what he was," agreed Anne of Cleves, glad the conversation seemed to be turning her way. "Yes, of course we were so full of praise for him at the time, even at the moment of our deaths, but then, we had to be. But he is no longer here, and we are. If he has taken the opportunity to leave his realm via a white light – which, according to Jane, he probably has – then he has left it unattended. We must claim it, all of us, together." She looked around at the five women, hoping that her speech and sentiments would be enough to convince them. She hadn't been entirely sure as she rehearsed, but it had flowed so easily, and now she just wanted to see their reactions.

The silence was deafening.

A whole minute passed without a word, feeling to Anne of Cleves like a thousand hours. Finally, it was broken.

"What is it, exactly, that you propose?" Katherine of

Aragon spoke quietly, but with confidence.

"Nothing quite so dramatic as you ladies might experience at the Tower," she nodded to Anne Boleyn and Katherine Howard. "But I have heard that you use your hauntings to further your own good reputations, rather than allowing people to think ill of you. I suggest the same for the rest of us. Some calm, gentle, peaceful hauntings of our graves, every now and then, to put ourselves back into the public mind. And, even if you do not like the idea of doing it yourself, I am sure that we can find willing participants to assist. After all, it need only be an approximation." She paused and looked at the group.

Jane Seymour nodded slowly. "St George's is such a beautiful chapel, a flicker here or there wouldn't be unexpected or harmful."

"Use the Queen's Closet as a vantage point," said Catherine Parr. "If you time it right, it could be very effective." Anne Boleyn and Katherine Howard murmured their agreement and encouragement.

As one, all five turned to Katherine of Aragon. Anne of Cleves knew they didn't need her permission, as such, but she was the most senior amongst them; even Anne, another grand European heiress, had to acknowledge Katherine's royal blood ran the thickest of them all. She dared to add a convincer.

"Even your daughter enjoys a hint of haunting now and then. I have seen it for myself, even if, I confess, she mainly haunts other spirits."

The former Spanish princess looked steadily at Anne of Cleves, then a hint of a smile played on her lips. "And I have met with Mary, Queen of Scots on many an occasion when she visits Peterborough. She is another who is keen on a good haunting. Often with my own child."

"Well, what say you?" Catherine Parr asked.

"I do not say I will make a significant contribution, but I agree with the notion," Katherine of Aragon said, carefully. "I have a strong, faithful group who still visit my grave, and I would not want them disturbed. But I do not see how a slight shimmer of visibility could hurt them, every so often."

Anne of Cleves couldn't help grinning. "You will see, I promise you, that the change will keep happening, if we keep working together. We will make a difference."

Katherine Howard smiled up at her older cousin. "And if you can make peace with Jane Boleyn, after all she did to you and your brother, surely there is hope for every relationship?"

Anne Boleyn looked at her predecessor. "Your Grace, none of us will do anything to harm the reputations of our collective; that has always been assured."

Katherine of Aragon nodded and smiled, then looked at Anne of Cleves. "Is this what you were hoping for, dear Anne, when you called us all together like this? The forming of a group, a sisterhood?"

"We have always been a sisterhood," replied Anne of Cleves. "Even if we did not admit it at the time."

"So, what happens now?" asked Jane, looking out of a nearby window at the exit-drawn drift of visitors began to make their way home for the day.

"I don't know," admitted Anne of Cleves. "But I would like to think we can meet again, here, or elsewhere?"

"You should come to the Tower," said Anne Boleyn. "We can show you all how to haunt in style, some proper spooking."

"One step at a time, I think, don't you?" said Anne of Cleves, gently. "But I did have one thought, of going to visit our current incumbent?"

The six women glanced around at each other and nodded, albeit some more keenly than others.

Anne of Cleves smiled. The day had worked out just as she had hoped after all. There was a long way to go, but they were heading towards the right path, at least. "Let's not leave it quite so long next time though, shall we, sisters?"

Kindred Spirits:
Leicester – Return of the King

A version of this story originally appeared in Grant me the Carving of my Name, *an anthology of short stories inspired by Richard III, released in 2018.*

As the doors of Leicester Cathedral closed for the final time that day, the ghost of Elizabeth Simpson sank into a chair in the south aisle.

"One of our busiest Saturdays for a while, I think," she said, not entirely sure who was about, but certain that somebody would be, whether she could see them or not. That was the thing with ghostly communities – transient groups in every way.

"I counted almost five hundred, I'm sure, from the ticks in the staff notebook." The deep, steady voice of her husband Samuel made Elizabeth jump.

"I wish you wouldn't do that," she scolded. "Over two hundred years of this, and you still insist on making me jump."

"Well, you shouldn't spend so long lost in your own thoughts," her husband retorted. "Anyway, we must keep our disagreements to ourselves; you never know who is around these days."

It was true. The cathedral had seen a resurgence in ghostly activity since the reinterment of King Richard III in March 2015. Ghosts who had been thought long gone appeared, out of the blue, at the nightly gatherings. Between these newer re-arrivals, and the increased visitor numbers amongst the living, some of the longer-term residents were unimpressed.

"Watch out, my dear, Whatton's on his way," Samuel said, nudging his wife. Elizabeth nodded at the approaching man, but didn't rise. She knew he hated that.

"Simpson," John Whatton said in greeting as he drew level with them. "My lady," he nodded stiffly to Elizabeth. "More Richard III fans crowding the place out today, I see. Honestly, you'd think the novelty would have worn off by now."

"Don't start all this again, Whatton," Samuel sighed. "Westley will be along at any moment, and between the pair of you, it's enough to drive any man back to his tomb."

"Or woman," Elizabeth added. Personally, she enjoyed the increase in activity. After all, there were so many interesting people buried in the cathedral, and a good number had stayed around. She glanced across the space, wondering if, and hoping that, Marie Bond would make an appearance that evening. At ninety-seven years old, Marie was the eldest regular resident of the cathedral, and the tales she could tell kept them all entertained – when she was in the mood.

To Elizabeth's delight, the elderly lady appeared, escorted as usual on the willing arm of young Susanna Peppin.

"Marie! So lovely to see you!" Elizabeth rose and greeted her friend and her companion, receiving a tut of derision from Whatton. She ignored him, showing Marie to a chair and ensuring the lady was comfortably settled. They had never managed to secure a permanent solution to the walking-stick problem for her, so human (or spectral) assistance was the best they could offer. Susanna never seemed to mind.

"Somebody thought they saw Richard's ghost outside in the square this afternoon. You haven't heard anything have you?" Marie asked of the group.

"Richard?" John Westley had arrived.

"Yes, Richard. The Third, obviously. Well? Anyone else see anything?"

Elizabeth shook her head. "I've been out and about most

of the day, albeit invisible. I would have seen him if he'd come inside."

"Typical," scoffed Whatton. "We are the ones who have stayed here, all these years. He visits – what? – once, since the funeral? And yet it's his ghost they all claim to see. We don't interfere with him and his friends at the Tower; how dare he disturb our days here?"

"But he doesn't, my dear man. I think that's rather the point," said Marie, rolling her eyes at Elizabeth.

"I just think it's a bit too much. He's nothing but a late-comer. He's been a resident for – what? – a matter of a few years? And yet he gets all the attention." John Whatton wasn't finished.

"Well, is it truly any wonder?" Marie snapped at him. "Apart from being of some interest to a few history students or distant relatives, what exactly do the rest of us have to offer? We should be grateful to have even just the bones of a king amongst us, keeping things lively."

"Hear, hear," seconded Elizabeth.

"Everyone, everyone!" John Herrick broke into the group's conversation.

"What is it, husband, why the commotion?" Marie demanded.

"He's here, it's true!"

"What?" the spirits demanded in unison.

"Richard. King Richard. With Queen Anne. He's come to visit …"

"If we do this, we do it entirely out of sight," said Queen Anne Neville, looking her husband directly in the eye. Second husband, if anyone wanted to be pedantic, but she didn't. She didn't like to think of her first husband Edward (the son of Henry VI), eternally glad the man's ghost had never chosen to try and visit her.

Richard turned to look up at the tower of Leicester Cathedral behind them.

"But I'm sure we were seen, so we might as well just carry on, surely? And so what if a few of my loyal fans spy me here or there?"

"Being seen for a moment by a cathedral resident is one thing, and harmless enough, but I don't want you causing any disruptions. I agreed to come with you if you swore there'd be no trouble. The first hint of it, and I'll be back on the next train out of here, back to London. Without you."

Anne smiled to herself as she saw Richard's shoulders drop. Whatever the reputation he had at the Tower, even after only a few visits to Westminster Abbey, she knew he was still the charming, gallant knight he had once been, and still a man of his word as a result. Battles and conspiracies hadn't completely erased that.

"Come on, don't you want to get going?"

Richard shook his head. "Not this evening. There's a fair amount to get through, and I don't want to rush." He paused. "I am glad you agreed to come with me. I've only been back briefly, and I wanted to see what the whole place was like now, a few years down the line."

"Don't get all soppy on me, Richard Plantagenet. I'm sure there are others who would have visited with you if you had asked, even other queens at that. So, if we're not starting now, what's the plan?"

"Well, according to the map," Richard consulted the pamphlet he'd managed to smuggle out of the visitor centre dedicated to him, disguised in a gust of wind as the automatic doors blew open earlier, "the tour should actually start at the Blue Boar Inn, so I thought we'd go there this evening, stay over, get a feel for the place, and make a start bright and early tomorrow morning."

"Is that even possible? Staying over I mean?" Anne raised an eyebrow.

"It's still a hotel. Well, I mean, there's still a hotel on the site. Not the same one, of course. There's bound to be an empty room. Then, tomorrow, we start at Bow Bridge. Again, not original, but still ..."

Anne tilted her head to one side, not immediately convinced by Richard's plan, but it was getting late, and even being able to pass through walls didn't make getting lost in a comparatively strange town an appealing option.

"Very well. Come on, let's see what we can find."

The next morning, having spent a comfortable night in the modern hotel – in between playing with the television and some gentle haunting of a few groups of drunks – Richard and Anne left via the glass automatic doors, leaving behind them the smell of cooking breakfast and light gossip. Consulting the map once again, the couple made their way through the square and across the traffic to the current Bow Bridge, a more modern replacement of the one Richard had crossed that fateful day back in 1485. Both fateful days, come to think of it.

"Honestly, that woman and her spurs story," he tutted. "Things hit bridges, it means nothing. And whatever that soothsayer might have said, my head did not hit the parapet on the way back."

Anne rolled her eyes. She'd worried this would happen. Everything was obviously going to be different, and plenty would most likely be wrong in her husband's eyes. Finding the old Leicester Castle, the next location on their journey, converted into a business school (part of the university), sent him off into another rant as he strode around the series of modern rooms, pointing out what should have been where. Eventually, she managed to usher him into the calm of the church of St Mary de Castro.

"This is better," said Richard, visibly relaxing.

The place was almost empty, their tour having reached the church before it was open to the public. Only a handful of volunteers were pottering about, getting the place open and ready for the day's visitors. The scent of incense hung heavy in the air, as Richard strolled across to a pile of leaflets and started flicking through.

"At least they have it mostly right," he said. "I did like this place, enjoyed worshipping here when I visited. And look, they've even noted it: *The last monarch to worship here*." He'd found the portrait of himself hanging on the wall. With a scowl, he noticed the portrait hanging next to it: Henry VI. "Just a shame there's such a strong Lancastrian presence."

Richard felt Anne approaching from behind, and knew it was pointless to think too negatively about how things were. Truth was, they were following his Walking Trail, not Henry VI's or Henry Tudor's, around places labelled with their links to him, and nobody else. That wouldn't be the case if nobody cared. And here he was, on a progress of sorts, Anne by his side, having agreed to join him for whatever reason he hadn't yet fully fathomed. After so long, he wouldn't have blamed her for turning him down, but what they'd had was slowly starting to return, thanks to their gradually more frequent trips. Even their venture to York had been a delight, if you ignored the arguments with locals and the fact that Henry Tudor had also been with them. He was courting his own wife, and both parties seemed to be enjoying it. Except, she was currently looking at a portrait of her former father-in-law. This would not do.

He coughed quietly, hoping to attract her attention, and help her note that he wasn't pleased with the attention she was paying Henry VI's portrait. As she turned, and made her way towards him, he quickly turned away, not wanting her to see he was troubled by her attention to Lancastrian portraits.

He felt her arm on his, and smiled.

"Shall we rest a while?"

They strolled through to the front of the church, and sat down, tucked out of the way in case visitors suddenly arrived. After an hour of sitting and enjoying the peace, watching the odd tourist make their way around the building, Richard was ready to move on. With a final glance, they passed back through the walls into Castle Yard, and turned towards the Turret Gateway. Here as well, he felt on solid ground. The area, although obviously modern in context, at least had a similar layout to that which he had remembered. The gateway was more crumbled, but he felt he knew where he was.

Reaching the main street, Richard paused for a moment,

before pulling himself up straight and looking at the building opposite. From what he could see, this was now another part of the university.

"Of course, the Church of the Annunciation is long gone, but apparently some of the original arches are still in the basement." Even he could hear the forced steadiness in his voice.

Without another word, he slipped through the walls, as Anne followed rapidly behind, only to pass straight through him as he froze just inches from the other side. He was staring into space, not focusing on his surroundings, not focusing on anything. Just blank.

"I can't. I thought I could, thought I could make light of it, but I can't," he said, his voice starting to crack. He shook his head, trying to rid himself of the image: his own corpse, lying on public display, the wounds of battle there for all to see. His humiliation.

Anne didn't reply, but wrapped him in her arms and pulled him close.

"It's OK," she said, after a long silence.

Richard nodded into her shoulder. He didn't want to move, but knew he couldn't stay in that building any longer.

"To the next gateway?" he mumbled.

Anne nodded, and pushed him gently away. "This is why invisible is better," she said, barely above a whisper.

"Right then." He turned and led the way back to the street. "A quick turn around the Newarke Gateway, then on to the main event, as it were?"

As they approached the area of the visitor centre, cathedral and Guildhall, Richard felt a weight pressing where his heart would have been. It hadn't been there at the start of the day, or when he'd visited briefly in the past, but today, having seen the rest of the tour, with all those memories flooding back, he was somehow more involved.

"Come on," encouraged Anne, reaching for his hand. "It'll be fine. And maybe a touch of gentle haunting wouldn't hurt."

Richard grinned. He knew he would get his way in the end. He always did. Even if 'the end' involved lying in a lost grave for a couple of centuries, then having the indignity of his feet being cut off by a wall and a carpark built over his head. Yes, he could play the long game. Battles and wars and all that.

The bells started to chime a call to service, as people began to mill about, catching up with each other in twos and threes. He stayed out of sight of the living. These weren't the right targets for a haunting. He would wait and find some suitable tourists later. He offered the crook of his elbow to Anne.

"Shall we attend the service?" he asked.

She replied by slipping her arm through his, and they flickered through the stone wall. To their surprise, a group of ghosts were waiting for them as they entered. The royal couple nodded their greeting, unsure initially what sort of response they would receive.

"Elizabeth and Samuel Simpson, Your Graces." A man spoke first, stepping forward, his wife alongside him in greeting. Others behind them nodded, a hint of nervousness about their reactions.

"Come to interfere, have you?" John Whatton butted into proceedings.

"No, why would you say that?" said Anne, hurriedly, before Richard could say a word.

Whatton didn't even bother to reply, instead walking off, deliberately turning his back on the Plantagenet pair.

"Well, what a reaction," she continued, looking to the Simpsons.

They shook their heads, almost in unison.

"Ignore him, Your Grace. Ignore all of us. Please, make yourselves at home, and do enjoy your visit. But please feel free to join us again later, should you wish."

The small welcome party vanished, each disappearing in their own direction.

"An interesting welcome," mused Richard, looking around the building properly, wondering who else might be around, and who they might encounter. "Come on, let's get started. I won't visit the tomb during the service; that doesn't feel right." They perched on seats at the back, being careful not to disturb anything as they did so.

For the duration, the pair sat calmly. The Church of England wasn't their denomination, but both enjoyed the peace that was so often lacking in their daily activities. As the final hymn drew to a close, Anne placed her hand over her husband's. He turned his over and squeezed hers in return. Yes, the day was going well.

The congregation began to disperse, the steady flow outward being gradually replaced by a trickle inward, as visitors realized the service was over, and the cathedral could once again be entered by tourists.

Richard's tomb was at the back, still protected by the strictest security of the velvet rope, in place during the service and not yet removed. People hovered on either side of the space, waiting to go in, whilst Anne and Richard, invisible to all, slipped through.

"It's beautiful," said Anne, taking Richard's hand again.

"It is," Richard agreed. "I mean, yes, it doesn't have the whole effigy thing going on, and some have argued it's a bit plain, but it's certainly striking. Simple and effective I think. A significant improvement on what I had to start with, and a lot more dignified than a carpark space!"

He had listened to and read all the discussion about where his mortal remains should have been located: here in Leicester, in Gloucester, in York, or (where kings had been buried for centuries) in Westminster Abbey. Standing beside the stone tomb here, at the heart of the cathedral, he was pleased to be in pride of place, his name and motto carved, resplendent and unmissable.

Finally, the rope was moved aside, and the line of tourists began to snake past, all quiet, respectful and calm. These still weren't the right people, Richard thought. Nor in the right place. He glanced about, and saw his target. A group of schoolchildren, being herded into the main door by a stressed-looking teacher. A few other adults were spread through the group, trying to keep things in order.

"See, I know where I am with a school party," he said, only half to Anne, as he slipped through the thick walls, across the sanctuary and around to the back of the group. As one of the cathedral volunteers gave an introduction to the site, and told them about Richard's discovery and reburial, he picked his victim, a small, quiet child at back of the group. As the volunteer reached the end of her talk, she smiled at the children and asked if they had any questions.

"Go on," Richard whispered. "Ask if there's a ghost."

The small boy he had selected spun around, eyes wide, but he would see nothing.

Richard chuckled to himself, then glanced at Anne to see whether she had decided to join him. She had not, but was smiling at him, gently shaking her head.

He continued around the group. For his next victim, he chose something different. A small girl, loitering at the back; her pigtails were just too much to resist, especially as there was nobody behind her she could blame. After emitting a small squeak, and being subsequently scolded, she hurried to the front of the column, staying as close to her teacher as possible.

After distracting a couple of the volunteers and adults, he returned to Anne, now sitting in St George's chapel, looking up at the carvings and stained glass windows.

"It's good to get it out of your system now and then," he said, joining her.

"On to the visitor centre, then?" she replied.

Richard nodded. This was going to be interesting.

He knew the layout from his previous visit, but that time, he hadn't felt up to going as far as seeing his original grave-site, or what they had done around the place in terms of exhibition and presentation. This time, with Anne at his side, he knew he had to do it. But he would do it properly, follow the route, see how things had been done, and enjoy – if that was the right word – the build-up to the site itself.

Ignoring the doors and crowds waiting patiently to pay

their entry fees, Richard and Anne made their way into the exhibition, stopping to watch the video which was just about to restart on a wall-sized screen, behind a mocked-up medieval throne.

"Now, before we go in, I don't want a running commentary of what you're not happy about, do you understand?" said Anne, instantly distracted by a representation of herself, walking on to the screen and giving her name to the watching group. "Well – well, I never. That's meant to be me! I didn't think I would feature."

"Ah, but of course you feature; you should be the star of the show," teased Richard, nudging her with his shoulder.

She shushed him, and they made their way into the exhibition proper.

To Anne's surprise, Richard managed to keep his own counsel throughout most of the exhibition. The history, after all, had been discussed and disputed for years; there was little point a ghost arguing with what was written now – what could he do about it anyway? It was the science that was fascinating. Yes, the story of how the dig had come about, and the physical side of actually finding his skeleton was interesting, but all those analyses? The fact that they could determine (with some accuracy, they both had to confess) what his diet had comprised, how tall he had been, and what sort of world he had inhabited – in Anne's and Richard's eyes, all that was close to witchcraft.

"All this can be told from our bones," said Richard, staring at the mock-up of his own skeleton, on display in the centre of the room.

"And that's just for now," Anne replied, hoping he wouldn't be distracted by the signs about fatal injuries and weapons of the day. "I mean, we would never have imagined them doing this in our day, but look how much has changed just in the last century. Who knows what else they might discover if they look at it all again in another couple of decades."

Finally, making their way downstairs, they approached the small, chapel-like area that enclosed his original grave, in the now famous car park.

Richard paused, still uncertain, only to find himself being urged on by Anne.

"You can do this, husband," she whispered, before smiling encouragement.

"Whether I can or I can't, I have to," he replied.

They stood at the entrance, waiting for a small group to leave; this was no place for a haunting. Seeing nobody about to follow them, Richard took Anne's hand, and stepped through the doorway.

The calm struck him first. Yes, it looked like a chapel, built over the small site, but somehow it felt like one too. With pale stone walls, low benches and high windows, it felt a positive space. Then he saw the glass. Rising up from the floor, right to the ceiling – the grave was encased entirely.

Slowly, avoiding looking at the guide seated to one side, Richard stepped forward, steadying himself.

He could do this. Of course he could.

The last time he had looked down on this grave, it had been surrounded by the buildings of Greyfriars, not yet topped with any monument, but covered in, with prayers still being said for his soul. He hadn't stayed long after his burial; he hadn't seen the point. London was where things were happening, London was where decisions were being made, so London was where he had gone – once he was used to his ghostly form.

The Tower of London had become home so quickly that he'd hardly travelled since, beyond the odd foray in the last couple of years. Being so far away, and with Anne by his side, he felt a strength he had lately occasionally found lacking.

"It's beautiful." Anne's voice broke into his train of thought. She moved up to the glass, then half a heartbeat later, jumped back in shock, staring at Richard.

"What is it?" he asked, moving forward to join her. Then

he saw it.

A projector, hidden in the top of the glass, created an image within the grave – one that was too perfect a depiction of Richard's skeleton for either of them to be comfortable with it.

"That's how he left you?" asked Anne, in a whisper.

"Yep. But we, well, I, would have done the same. It was never just about the battle, was it? What you did next was always just as important."

"But – when you compare what we had – in terms of our graves ... I'm sorry." She reached for his hand.

"It's amended now, that's all that matters. I've got my grave, pride of place, right in the heart of the cathedral, my name and motto given their dues."

Richard watched the projection fade in and out a few more times before speaking again.

"I'm glad we came back, but I think this is it now. Onwards and upwards."

"Not your white light? You wouldn't leave us all?" There was the hint of a shake to Anne's voice.

"Leave? Who mentioned leaving? Well, leaving here, yes, but that's it. No, I don't intend to go anywhere anytime soon; things are just starting to get fun, after all. Being here, it was important, but this is the past for me now. They've found me, reburied me, and my reputation is turning around quite nicely." He put his arm around her shoulders. "Me and you – how about we head back to London, to our respective homes, but on the way, we make ourselves a plan? Think of all the places we can visit, the fun we can have; it'll be as if the last five hundred odd years never even happened. How about it?"

Anne pulled away from Richard, and looked him in the eye.

"Go travelling?"

"A royal progress, or at least a couple more visits like those we've had so far. I hear the Scots Queen is planning one too. And we can't let her have all the fun now, can we?"

Anne smiled. "A royal progress. Yes, I like that idea. All

right, I'm in."

Richard clapped his hands together and grinned. "An excellent decision, I assure you. So, back to London? It's time we were planning."

With a final glance at the projected image of his skeleton in his cramped, undignified grave, Richard and Anne made their way out of the exhibition, nodded to two of the cathedral's ghosts, loitering at the great wooden door, and made their way towards the station.

Kindred Spirits:
The Jewel of the Wall

"*Tablet 291.*" Claudia Severa read the small printed sign aloud to her sister. "*The earliest known example of a woman's handwriting in Britain.*"

Sulpicia Lepidina sighed and rolled her eyes. "By sheer fluke, that's all. If I'd written to you, rather than sending a messenger, they could be looking at my handwriting now, not yours. After all, the interpretation makes it clear that there were plenty of letters; this was not a rare thing."

"Oh, dear sister, do not be bitter. I'm sure some of your letters exist somewhere, somehow, under all of this. After all, the great wife of Vindolanda's commander; you wrote so many notes and letters, not just to me." Claudia waved her arm around, vaguely indicating the size of the Roman fort they were standing in, the letters currently on loan to the fort where they had been discovered.

Sulpicia huffed. She knew the chances of more tablet letters turning up were remote. After all, she was the one living at the great fort of Vindolanda, a location which had been relatively well-protected and preserved over the years. Claudia's home was long gone, no trace remaining; her replies to her sister had likely been destroyed, by people, time or weather, centuries ago.

She forced a smile onto her face. After all, this was not the first run-through of this argument, and she strongly doubted it would be the last. Almost two thousand years now, the sisters had been together. Plenty of time for arguments, and especially since that wretched tablet had been found in the 1970s.

Still, she thought, they had chosen to stay together,

despite their differences.

AD100, it had been, when her sister wrote that note. They had each lost their husbands soon after, and their own lives not far behind. Still, 'life' as a ghost wasn't too bad. There had always been plenty to watch along the Wall, all those comings-and-goings, as the Romans left, the various tribes, Vikings, Normans, came and went, vicious raids by reivers, skirmishes over the land, and finally, peace.

Now, their only 'invaders' were the tourists, visiting the sisters' wall, hiking along its length, stopping to admire the various forts or other buildings which still dotted the ancient border between England and Scotland.

There was nothing more magical than the Wall at night, the moon bathing everything in its silver glow, and the flicker of a Roman guard, choosing just the right moment, as late-night walkers took one last glance up across the moorland.

Plenty of Romans, from all sectors of the community, still spent their time along the route. They just chose who got the chance to see them...

Kindred Spirits:
Eurostar

Queen Mary glanced up at the platform clock; another ten minutes had ticked by, and the train showed no sign of leaving. Half an hour late, and the other passengers were starting to get restless. Watches were checked, as though repeating the action would somehow solve the problem. Tea and coffee were being served for her fellow first-class travellers to try and placate them, as the dulcet tones of the French-accented guard finally announced that they would be leaving 'in a few moments'.

After yet another ten minutes, the train moved.

Leaning back in her seat as she was carried out of London, through the suburbs, then out into fields, Mary sat, content to let the world pass her by. Champagne was the next treat, as she heard the pop and fizz enjoyed by her companions. Even without refreshments, this was a positive luxury compared to 'the bad old days' as she and her friends now labelled them.

Ships which felt as though they would collapse with the next large wave, tiny tenders ferrying you to shore, rough hands heaving you from gangplank to quayside. Yes, travelling under the Channel was far more comfortable than travelling over it.

With nothing else to occupy her time, Mary focused her attention on her destination: her beloved Paris. The Louvre, the Palais Royal; she mentally ticked off all the old haunts she was already looking forward to seeing again. She'd visited plenty of times before, yet, somehow, this felt different. More formal, perhaps, having sent word ahead.

Mary had always been a planner by nature, but never with Paris, preferring to appear unannounced, not minding who she did – or didn't – see. This time, though, she did care. King Francis II of France and Mary Seton had both been sent word of her intended visit, and if the dead could have butterflies, Mary's were currently on a rollercoaster around where her stomach would be.

Husband? Or friend? Or maybe both husband and friend? Who did she truly most want to see on the platform at Gare du Nord? One, both, or neither? Whichever turned up, they would make an odd pairing. Mary, at 44, would be met by either a 16-year-old boy, or a 73-year-old nun.

Death played tricks on you like that. The Scots Queen forced herself to lean back in her seat as they entered the blackness of the tunnel. Her travel companions were now dining on what looked to be fine cuisine indeed. That was another cruel trick of death: she could smell their lunch, but was unable to consume even the tiniest morsel. And she was heading to Paris, with the most heavenly cakes and pastries in the world. Mary smiled as she thought of how her friend Janet, notoriously sweet-toothed, would have hated it.

Needing a break from her own thoughts, Mary sought refuge in sleep, letting the carriage motion gently soothe her eyes shut. It didn't help; her dreams were just as restless.

It was a delay-free journey, this ride through time, as Mary's mind made its way through her life, playing the 'what if?' game. It was never a healthy way to spend any length of time. She thought of the young man who might be waiting to greet her. If he had lived, who knew what they could have had in Northern Europe? Their son might not have been a James – more likely a Henry, after his French grandfather – but he would still have inherited Elizabeth I's English throne, combining the ultimate trio of Scotland, France and England. And it would all have been through her.

She'd been through this before. She knew, deep down, that part of her ongoing historical celebrity was down to the very fact that poor Francis had died so young. A queen who married, settled down, had a son and did exactly what society expected of her rarely went down in history. Case in point: over the years she had met both Anne Boleyn and Jane Seymour, and look at the different celebrity status fate had dealt each of them in death.

"Marie!"

Mary's ears pricked at her French name, but it was pure coincidence, as a passenger opposite answered her phone, now they were out of the dark, and speeding through the French countryside. Gare du Nord was getting closer. Another reason why things were better these days. If you're going to spend a whole journey worrying to yourself, you may as well use the fastest mode of transport available to you.

This is why she travelled so much: creating plenty of other things to fill her thoughts, stopping any single issue becoming too dominant.

By now, the outskirts of Paris were starting to thicken outside the window – the hours had flown by. Mary smiled as the great Sacré Cœur loomed into view. She may have missed it in life, but she had loved visiting in death, drinking in the view of the city which had been her own capital for a painfully short time.

"I would have made a good Queen of France, given longer." Mary dared to raise her voice to an out-loud whisper. "You would have made a better Queen of England than Elizabeth," she told herself, this time in silence. "But enough of them both," a whisper again. "You did make a legendary Queen of Scots."

They were on the final approach to Gare du Nord, or 'Paris North' as one of the guards kept insisting on translating it to in his announcements. It just didn't hold the same level of romance in English.

Mary kept her eyes straight ahead as they reached the platform. Finally, as the train shuddered to a halt, she knew who she wanted to be waiting for her. Not bothering with the door, the passageway now crowded as people fetched cases down from the racks and made their way to the ends of the carriage, the Scots Queen simply exited sideways, directly onto the platform. Pressing against the side of the train, she avoided the living, not wanting to send shivers down anyone's spines today to alert them to her presence.

Waiting for the throng to clear, she glanced up the emptying platform to where a dwindling group still waited for their straggling friends, families and colleagues to make their way up the length of the train to meet them. The sight caused a smile to creep across her face.

There was no sign of Francis.

Or Mary Seton.

The faint spirit of a former station-master raised his arm in greeting to the queen, but neither husband nor friend were to be seen.

"It's for the best," she said out loud, not caring this time who might hear. "It is for the best."

It was time to stop looking back, Mary thought, as she strolled up the platform. The last of the passengers were now off the train, and the cleaning staff had started their sweep through the carriages. For a moment, she let herself think of the conversations she might have had with either of her potential greeters, but found herself drawing an awkward blank after the initial 'Hello' was done with. They had all changed so much in the intervening years. Or should have done, anyway. What would a woman in her forties, who had spent almost half her life in captivity, say to a husband young enough to be her son, or a woman who had given up a life of glamour for that of religion? She couldn't think of anything. She doubted that either would appreciate tales of hauntings down Edinburgh's closes, or the teasing of Queen Elizabeth.

An image of Janet Douglas, Lady Glamis, and Sir William Kirkcaldy, the lady's handsome knight, flashed through Mary's mind. The pair were always such good company during her time in Edinburgh, and they were finally planning the royal progress around the great castles and stately homes of Scotland that had been on the cards for years. Perhaps that was where her future lay – in new friendships, rather than old ones. Well, hardly new after more than four centuries, but certainly newer than her French connections. Those two enjoyed a good haunting, when the mood took them. They shared her sense of humour, as well as her troubles.

Now outside the station, Mary observed the comings and goings of the crowd: everyone heading somewhere, everyone on their way to the next destination, whether rushing or dawdling.

"It must be the same for me," she declared, pulling herself up to her full height. No more antagonising Gloriana, however great the temptation. When she returned to Westminster, she would do so out of friendship for her cousin, Queen Mary I, or to see her beloved son, James VI. And as for Paris, she could take in the sites solo just as easily as in company. After all, there were plenty of local ghosts to share the time of day with. Paris had some of the finest cemeteries in Europe. When it came to their spiritual residents, it would be a delight to spend some time in their company.

Confident in her decision, Queen Mary nodded to herself, and made her way into the streets of Paris.

Kindred Spirits:
Père Lachaise

"I finally got around to tidying the tomb," said Héloïse, as she joined Peter at the table, just opposite the walls of Père Lachaise Cemetery.

Her husband sighed and dropped his head into his hands. "I am so sorry, I got distracted."

"Again. Honestly, Peter, I've been asking you for the last fortnight. The staff around here are lovely, but it's such a large site, after all."

"They always seem to manage to keep their celebrities' tombs clear enough," Peter complained. "You never see litter clogging up Jim Morrison's grave."

"No dear, I know. Nor Edith Piaf's, or Oscar Wilde's; you have mentioned this." She patted his hand, and looked longingly at the coffee cups, abandoned by the table's previous occupants. Meanwhile, Peter was still complaining.

"But we're the oldest in there, by far – the least they could do is show a little respect for their elders."

Héloïse leaned back in the chair and closed her eyes, imagining the warmth of the early-morning sun, bringing a glow to her cheeks. She didn't mind the others getting more attention. She enjoyed the peace and quiet that their little corner of the cemetery afforded them. They had gone through enough in life, and even the first few centuries of death; calm and tranquillity was all that Héloïse wanted now. But her husband had other ideas. He always had done.

"I'm still glad you waited for me," she said, her train of thought having delivered her to the day of her death, at the Oratory of the Paraclete.

"What else would I have done, my love?"

"Well, you were, are, a theological philosopher, after all – I could never have blamed you for wanting to move on and explore what came next," Héloïse replied.

"This bit of 'next' is quite enough for me, I assure you," said Peter, taking her hand in his across the table. Even lacking flesh and blood, the sense was still there, just. "But speaking of next, you have reminded me – the next philosophy debate is this evening, and I am nowhere near prepared."

"But you have had a month? Really, Peter, they will throw you out again if you don't focus." Despite the frustration in her voice, she stroked the back of his hand with her thumb as she replied.

"Well, 'they' wouldn't't," argued Peter, "but Comte is desperate for an excuse to take over."

Héloïse sighed. Auguste Comte had been trying for years to oust her husband from his position as lead philosopher in the cemetery. "Then don't give him that excuse. Go on – it is only just turning nine o'clock, you have all day, and I smuggled you in fresh pen and paper just last week."

Peter turned and looked as though he was about to argue with her; in that moment all Héloïse could see, in the shape of his eyes and the curve of his lips, was the face of their son, a petulant toddler, trying to avoid being sent to his tutor. Poor little Astrolabe. She forced the image from her mind before it got too much; she still couldn't accept why their son had never joined them in the afterlife. They could still have been a happy family.

Peter was still protesting. "But we were going to take a stroll, maybe go for a boat ride?"

"Peter Abelard. The Seine and its boats have been there since the day we met, for millennia before, and will be there tomorrow, and for plenty more tomorrows to come. Besides, won't it be more fun to cruise along the river whilst you share the tale of your latest debating victory?" She smiled at him.

Peter glanced back at the cemetery's great walls.

"Germain has been particularly imaginative this last few times, when she can tear herself away from that wretched cyclist."

"Laurent Fignon is a national hero; do not be jealous. Besides, he is courting fair Rosalie," Héloïse replied. "Not that I am one to gossip, of course."

"The courtesan?" Peter's eyes lit up. "The first woman in history officially recorded as a 'dumb blonde', and the cyclist has picked her over the great intellect of Sophie Germain? Oh, this is priceless." He was already on his feet. "My love, I shall bid you farewell, and return triumphant this evening." Raising her hand to his lips in a goodbye, he turned and vanished.

Héloïse chuckled to herself. Even after all this time, she could still best her supposedly quick-minded husband. Rosalie Duthe was still a grand woman, despite her aforementioned nickname and reputation, but at over eighty, she was no match for Fignon, and no competition for Sophie. One day, Héloïse thought, she really should take part in the competitions and debates herself. But she had her own duties.

The deep hum of an engine caught her attention, as a hearse manoeuvred slowly into the cemetery.

"And so, to work," said Héloïse, half-aloud, as she made her way to the freshly-opened tomb, to greet the new arrival.

Kindred Spirits:
York Revisited

It wasn't black.

That's what Detective Inspector Duncan Clarke found himself thinking, as he stood, watching his own body gradually losing heat as his lifeblood stopped flowing.

But it wasn't white either.

He wasn't sure what he had expected, if he had expected anything at all, but he had perhaps assumed that death was either black nothingness, or a bright, glowing white.

Instead, it was strangely the same as things had been in life.

So, was he a ghost now? The thought was so odd to him that for a moment, he couldn't even register sorrow. Then it hit him.

He was dead.

He had been murdered. Him, DI Clarke, brutally slain in the line of duty. What would his parents think? What would his partner say? Would Sloan be able to catch his killer?

Could he help?

He had watched, and loved, *Randall and Hopkirk (Deceased)*; could there be a second career for him? For now, though, the distance between the killer and the crime scene was growing with every moment he wasted time thinking. Enjoying his new-found skill of passing through walls, Duncan hurried into the corridor, down the sweeping staircase, and out into the small entrance way beyond. Empty.

"Are you alright, sweetheart?"

"Wh... what? You can see me?"

The petite, pretty brunette in what looked like Regency

costume smiled at him.

"I can, my dear – we're all in the same boat, as it were. I'm Kate; welcome to the afterlife." She reached out a hand, and didn't seem too put out when he didn't take it.

"You, you're dead too? Wait, did you see somebody run out of here? Towards town perhaps?" Despite everything, Duncan's instinct kicked in.

"Sorry, no. I just got a sense something was wrong, so I came along to check, and found you."

As Kate moved closer, Duncan instinctively backed away.

"Don't worry, I won't hurt you, and if you'd rather speak to a man about things, I can fetch somebody?"

"You make it sound so casual."

"I'm sorry, it's been a couple of centuries for me, so there's nothing much can shock me now. Anyway, come on, let's get out of this place. It never does anyone any good to hang around their own corpse, especially not with forensics and all sorts making their presence felt." She looked at him more closely. "Why were you in there anyway?"

It was only then he remembered exactly what had happened: the chase through York, becoming separated from the rest of the team, heading towards the river, the museum, then, well, that. The string of thefts had been turning gradually worse, more violent, but this had been a step further than any of them had imagined. He hoped it was just an accident, that the guy who had turned on him had done so only out of fear, seeing the law closing in after having evaded them for so long.

"I'm a detective; I need to be here, to help. I can just tell my partner what happened, can't I?" He gave what he hoped was a hopeful expression, and smiled. Her frown didn't help.

"A detective? Well, this is a first for me. But I'm sorry, again, I really am; it cannot be that easy. If it was, you police would all be out of work soon enough, wouldn't you? I mean, we ghosts could just keep watch, and tell somebody exactly what happened, whenever a crime was committed."

"It would certainly help our stats. Mind, I'm not doing too badly on my own, I'll have you know; I've only got one unsolved murder. Poor Xanthe."

"Xanthe?"

Duncan was surprised at the shock in her voice. Everyone in the city knew about Xanthe and her fate.

"Yes, you must have heard about it. Young lass, worked at the Jorvik, killed after closing up one night, and the whole area a complete mess the next morning. Swords, the pathologist reckoned. Swords? Who even uses swords? What?" Duncan noticed Kate's wide eyes.

"Nothing. Nothing at all. I mean, yes, of course I heard about it. We all did. Such a terrible tragedy, and in our own backyard, so to speak. Look, let's get you away, please. There's a few of us meeting up in the Barley Hall this evening. Why don't you join us?"

Duncan looked back at the building, knowing that by now his body would have lost every last trace of warmth. How could he just walk away, leave the scene of a crime, leave a body, HIS body? "Can we at least alert the authorities somehow, so they find me? I mean, they don't even know where I chased the guy to – it could be hours before some poor soul finds me tomorrow morning as they open up for the day, or even Monday." It was a Saturday night, after all. Panic threatened to overtake him, as the reality of the situation sank in. He had discovered plenty of dead bodies in his life, but for somebody else to find him just felt wrong, somehow.

Kate smiled at him, and reached for his hand, not letting him slip away this time. "I'll get the Duke on to it as soon as we see him." Not giving him any further choice, she pulled him away and into town.

'The Duke', Duncan was told as he entered the Barley Hall's upper floors with Kate, referred to Richard Plantagenet, the 3rd Duke of York (the original 'Grand Old Duke of York'). The Duke was currently deep in conversation with a handful of other spirits, and seemed to be discussing a planned trip away.

"Look, we can go over this again and again, but at the end of the day, we're leaving in a week, and that is final. It's already been six months; what can the hold-up possibly be this time?" He glared at an older woman sitting across from him. "Margaret?"

She held his gaze for a few seconds, then blinked and looked down at her hands, folded in her lap. "I'm sorry, it's just, it's nerves, I suppose. I've never travelled so far."

"If you dare suggest the roads aren't safe, I'll hold up our party myself," another ghost joked, as he pulled up the black face-mask which hung around his neck, smirking at two other men beside him as he did so, sharing a quiet laugh before that was quashed with a stare from the Duke.

"It's alright, Margaret," said another kindly-looking lady in a similar dress to Kate's, putting her arm around the older woman's shoulders. "Ignore him. Kate and I will be with you the whole time, us and Xan—"

"Awen!"

Duncan started, as Kate's greeting cut directly across Awen's words.

"Sorry, everyone, this is Detective Inspector Duncan Clarke – a policeman, obviously – who has just had a rather unfortunate encounter with the gentleman he was trying to apprehend."

A sea of faces turned as one, each with varying degrees of greeting and welcome. The Duke was first to rise.

"Has the body been reported? We don't want any more unfortunate incidents like last time."

"I was hoping you could see to that? I got Duncan as far away as possible first. The body is in the upstairs offices of the library, oh! A body in the library; I hadn't even thought of that before now. Why were you chasing him into the library?"

"Because that's where he ran. But you're right, he opened the door; he must either work there, or have stolen a key earlier somehow."

"No, he cannot work there," said Awen. "We know most

of the staff there from sitting in on events; nobody strikes me as the type who would kill."

"Unless you were really late taking your books back," joked one of the three men, setting them off smirking again.

"Guy, is that helping?" Awen shoved him in the ribs.

"Aye, Fawkes, enough," snarled the Duke.

"Sorry, Guy, Fawkes? What have I wandered into here?" Duncan stopped and finally looked around at the group, a mismatch of ages, periods and styles. They must all be ghosts, of course they must be, but who were they?

"We should do introductions," said the Duke. He began, explaining his role in the city as an attempt to help keep peace amongst the other ghosts. "We didn't do too well at the end of last year; not sure if you picked up on anything odd going on?"

"Well, we did, now you mention it. Wait, all that strangeness – it was all you? Why?"

"It wasn't us, not directly. Hotspur, Harry Hotspur." One of the group which contained Guy Fawkes stepped forward. "There was an issue with one of poor Saint Margaret's priests, which got out of hand, and ended up involving Romans, Vikings, out-of-towners, and ultimately us. It's resolved now, you'll be glad to know. Everything, well, mostly everything, was sorted out peacefully."

"Except Xanthe. I know you almost said her name earlier, and Kate went strange when I mentioned her earlier. I am a detective, and a good one, I'll have you know. What aren't you telling me?" Duncan looked around the rest of the group, who had introduced themselves, before turning to the young woman in modern clothing. She could have been his niece.

"I'm Xanthe," she said, standing up and shyly offering her hand for him to shake.

"You? You're my only unsolved murder case," said Duncan, stumbling as Kate guided him to a seat. "I'm so sorry."

"It's not your fault; I'm afraid I was rather 'unsolveable' I suppose."

"But, who? How? I mean, a *sword*?"

Xanthe looked across at the Duke, who nodded and picked up the tale.

"Hotspur said it got out of hand. There was a bloody street-battle across the city. The whole place was a mess. Trouble had been stirred up, which we were trying to put down, but ultimately, it became a running fight throughout the centre, and spilled down into Coppergate. Poor Xanthe here had been closing up for the night, after an evening event, and at one point, when Vikings and Romans were fully tangible, mid-fight... Well..." He waved his hand, as though still struggling to find the words, even after all this time. Xanthe smiled shyly at him in reassurance.

Duncan stared at her. This was too strange, beyond too strange. Had other detectives had to face this, meeting with their failures in the afterlife? Was this some sort of punishment? This was all getting too much. "Even knowing, there's nothing I can do now, is there?"

Kate shook her head. "What would happen if you even tried? You cannot just walk into your old office, appear and tell them you've solved your final case. Even if they didn't run screaming at the sight of you, the story is so fantastical. And let's imagine for a moment they stayed, and listened, and even believed you, there can't be any justice, can there?"

"Even if you tried, ghosts tend to be tricky to lock up."

"Guy! You. Are. Not. Helping." Awen punctuated every word with a shove. "Go away and haunt somebody. You too, Turpin, Hotspur; there's bound to be a ghost tour kicking off somewhere soon. If you must be annoying, annoy somebody who will at least enjoy it."

Duncan started at the name Turpin, and looked more closely at the man Awen had spoken of. He did have a hint of the rogue about him, but it couldn't be, could it? Although, it would explain his jest about holding up their party earlier.

Either way, Kate's glare was enough to shame the three men into leaving, Guy giving Awen the briefest of kisses on the cheek before they dropped through the floor into the space below.

"Don't worry," Kate continued. "They enjoy a good haunting; no grudges get held here for long these days. Not after last year. We all make much more of an effort to get along these days."

Duncan couldn't focus. That evening, he had left home with the sole intention of helping catch the criminals who had been making his and his team's lives miserable – and now, here he was, chatting to a roomful of ghosts as though it was the most natural thing in the world. This was ridiculous. And infuriating. And worse than that, he now seemed to be in the middle of a social gathering, all intent on not letting him resolve anything. He had to get out and try to make sense of everything.

"I'm sorry, I can't think straight just now. Please, just make sure somebody finds me, the old me, and let me at least sit in on the discussions? I don't know what's going on; I don't even know if I believe you're all real. I need to get home." He stopped abruptly. "My parents. I have to see them; they don't know about this. They need to know about this." Duncan was aware of the panic in his voice, but was no longer interested in hiding it.

Suddenly, Xanthe was beside him properly, gripping his arm. "You need to take your time, and be careful here. Think; you cannot just go barging in and see them – it would be too great a shock."

"But... but I live with them. This... this will break their hearts. It'll break mine."

The remaining ghosts exchanged the briefest of glances.

"Come on. I'll go with you," said Xanthe. "I'm the one who has been through this the most recently, so I'm the best-placed to get you through it. I visited my parents after Christmas, not straight after my... incident, and it isn't easy not to intervene." She smiled over at Kate and Awen. "Luckily, I had two wonderful friends to help me through it, and now it's my turn to do the same for somebody else."

The detective could do nothing but follow, as the young woman whose murder he had tried so hard to solve now walked alongside him, chattering away as he explained where he lived, only fifteen minutes' stroll from the city centre. As they approached his front door, she paused.

"You know you can't do anything. I mean, they won't even know you're dead yet, the Duke will only just have phoned in about you – some sort of anonymous tip-off, I'd imagine – so it'll take a while for everything to get sorted, identify you and so on. And believe me, it isn't wise to go barging in, even when they do know."

"Have your parents seen you?" Duncan asked. He could picture them, on the local news, in the Minster at her funeral, walking in and out of the police station as he and his colleagues had done their best to find the person who stole their daughter from them. His own parents were going to be the same now. Although, at least, his murderer was very much in the land of the living; his colleagues stood a better chance than he had done at bringing the killer to justice.

"They have, but not obviously. In my old room, there's a mirror that used to be my gran's. I sometimes find my parents sitting in the room, and I make a brief appearance in the reflection. Only for a moment, out the corner of an eye, you know, nothing too blatant. I don't want them thinking I'm haunting them as some lost soul: I want them to see it as comfort, not retribution or guilt, you know?"

Duncan nodded. "We have a huge old mirror in the lounge, that goes back a couple of generations. Perhaps I could steal your idea, after a while I mean? Maybe you could help me?" He needed somebody to help him through this; he wasn't sure he was strong enough to resist interfering.

"Of course I'll help you. This is a horrible situation for everyone, but we'll get you through it. All of us will. The Duke, Hotspur, Fawkes and Turpin, and Awen and Kate; they're a lovely bunch." She brightened for a moment. "They're taking me to London shortly, next week in fact.

That's what we were discussing when you arrived. London, the long way."

"London?"

"Yup. We're having a bit of an adventure, taking in some of their old haunts from life, as well as death, eventually ending up at Windsor Castle. I'm going to meet kings and queens, can you believe it?"

"You sound almost… happy?" Duncan couldn't get his head around the idea. They were discussing going on holiday?

She paused for a moment, deep in thought. "Of course I'm not happy to be dead. Who would be? That would be ridiculous. But, it happened, and I don't know, I guess this is better than there simply being nothing, isn't it?" She laughed at Duncan's confused expression. "Don't worry, they haven't brainwashed me! It doesn't work like that. But yeah, if it has to be this way, then I'm at peace with it. And my parents seem to be ok, which is important. Now, come on, let's see what happens here. The Police might be arriving soon to let them know, and I don't want you to see that."

He knew she was right, and that they needed to be away well before his colleagues arrived, but he suddenly felt the need to see his parents now, as they were, without knowing anything was wrong. Oddly, they were still up, sitting in the flickering light of the television, watching one of their favourite subtitled detective dramas, sunny Sicily by the looks of it. Duncan had got them hooked on it all, once he stepped into his policing life. The two ghosts slipped through the walls and into the back of the living room. There was no chatter going on between the older couple, but then, both were intently watching the screen, reading the text which flashed up, telling them the story. It could have looked a lonely scene, the two of them, sitting in the half-dark, not speaking, but there were subtle points, showing this was a happy home. The way his mother reached for his father's hand at a tense moment in the drama, and how he responded with a gentle squeeze of her fingers. Duncan blinked, scared that tears would start to flow too quickly. Could ghosts cry? He certainly felt as though he was about to.

A squeeze of his own hand brought his attention back to Xanthe. "Come on, we should go. You can come back tomorrow, or the next day, once the dust has settled, and we'll come up with some sort of sign, to let them know everything's alright."

Duncan nodded. "But is this it now? How long do I stay here?"

"Well," Xanthe looked upwards as she was thinking. "If your body is found, then, actually, I suppose it depends how quickly they identify you…"

"No, no, I mean, 'here', as in, dead?"

"Oh. Oh, that can be anything, apparently. Some people get offered a white light, a chance to move on, to go onto whatever comes next, but the thing is, nobody knows what exactly that is, so a lot of people stay here, as you can see."

"Have you had your chance?"

Xanthe shook her head. "But I'm staying put regardless. Like I said, I'm happy enough here, and yes, the next step might be lovely, but what if it's not? What if it's nothing, and I've given up what is actually quite entertaining in the here and now? I'm going to take my chances and stay here, with this lot, for a while at least."

Duncan nodded. In the distance, he heard police sirens starting up. Something was happening. Maybe they had found him. "That could be us."

"Come on, out of the way; it might not be long until they get here now. We'll head back to Barley Hall, and then see where you want to be in the morning. Most people find somewhere to be their home, of sorts, and we'll take it from there."

Without seeing an alternative, Duncan allowed Xanthe to lead him away, and back towards the city centre. It was strange, walking around the places he knew so well, and yet, not being there. He had done plenty of night-time walking, both for work and simply to help him relax at night, as a means to switch his brain 'off' in the evening, but this was strange. As a group of late-night partygoers staggered across the square in front of them, he instinctively reached an arm out to pull Xanthe behind him, in case the group got rowdy as they passed, then realised that it simply didn't matter any more. There was nothing this gang could do to hurt either him of them now.

Having realised what he had tried to do, Xanthe found his hand again and squeezed it. "I think you'll be best off staying around here for a while. You know the city as well as any of us, and who knows, perhaps some law and order might do us some good."

He went to argue, then – as though to prove her point – another group of what Duncan initially assumed to be drunks meandered up from the direction of the Minster. He was about to say something when he saw that they weren't drunks, but Roman soldiers.

Turning to Xanthe, he raised an eyebrow in question.

She shrugged. "Welcome to the real afterlife."

Kindred Spirits:
Windsor Castle

Some buildings, however many times you visit them, always have the power to impress when they first come into view.

Even ones you've lived in, mused the ghost of Richard III, as he and his motley crew of friends and relations turned the corner to be confronted with the mighty Windsor Castle's exterior walls. It had changed significantly since their day, with the town grown even more now, tourists bustling about, and so much more noise, but it was still a commanding view.

"Which way in then?" asked Richard's brother George, as they surveyed the heavy stonework. "Easy, or traditional?"

"I am not sloping into my former stronghold as though I have no right to be there," replied Richard. "Besides, we learned our lesson in York – royal visitors use royal doorways. We'll go in the main gate, and head straight to St George's."

"Just a minute." The deep voice of their father made both men turn. The 3rd Duke of York stood, flanked by Queens Anne Neville and Elizabeth of York. "With or without warning, this might not be the most gracious of welcomes. Richard, have you even seen your brother since you died? Edward might not be happy, if you catch my meaning?"

Richard tensed. He knew exactly what his father meant. Reuniting the three 'suns of York' may not, in hindsight, have been the brightest idea he had ever had. Still, if he could find a way to be civil with the usurper Tudor, he could do this.

A thought struck him. "Come to think of it, what about Tudor's brat of a son? Is he here?"

His wife stepped forward. "I spoke to Anne of Cleves after their little gathering at Hampton Court, and she assures me not. Surely Ms Boleyn reported the same to you?"

Richard smiled, relieved. Of course Anne had told him; he had simply been too preoccupied to take it in.

The rest of the party were starting to grow restless.

"Come on, Uncle. I want to see my parents, even if you don't." Without waiting for any further discussion, Elizabeth of York marched off in the direction of the main gates, the rest of the group falling into line behind her. Richard hung back for a moment, until his wife caught his gaze.

"Come on Richard, you can't back out now – we've been seen." She nodded up to the walls, where a mismatched band of soldiers was looking down on them. She reached for his hand as they hurried to catch up with the others.

"Fine, fine, but..." he looked around, "send somebody on ahead, to St George's, won't you? I don't want any surprises." He looked at his niece, knowing she also remembered the trip to York, and would see to it. In that moment, he was glad the rest of the visiting York party had agreed to let them do this initial visit on their own, without the likes of Fawkes or Turpin loitering in the background. He was sure they would all be having a good enough time of things back in the city.

"Alright, who is up for haunting duties today?" Edward IV surveyed the group of ghosts lined up in front of him.

"I'll take the Henry VIII role again, if nobody else is interested," offered Charles Brandon, the sovereign's greatest friend in life, and happily, of a similar enough build to act as a shadowy figure, haunting St George's, when he chose to.

Edward nodded, smiling at his now friend. He knew it still amused Brandon that Henry VIII's tomb was nowhere near as grand as the monarch had originally intended.

"And I shall go and be Elizabeth I for the morning," said Elizabeth Woodville, smiling at her husband.

"As long as nobody is pretending to be me."

The resident spirits turned as one as the sound of a new voice entering their discussion.

"William!" Edward bounded across the great chequered floor of the church to greet his friend, pulling him into a great bear hug.

"Hastings, welcome." The greeting from Edward's wife was not quite so enthusiastic, the king noted.

"What are you doing here, my friend? Is anyone with you?"

"Edward, I am merely the advance party, sent ahead by your charming daughter, so that we can make our presence known. We are quite a group today, I'll confess." William, Baron Hastings, stooped to formally kiss Queen Elizabeth's hand. "What a treat it shall be, to see three of England's most beautiful queens, gathered together."

"Three queens?" Elizabeth's eyes narrowed.

Edward saw the threat first, but was too taken aback to do anything about it.

"Hello, Elizabeth." Anne Neville stood with her niece, Edward's daughter, over the top of the latter's son's grave.

Edward didn't have time to worry about what would happen when mother, daughter and aunt came together; he had just spotted his brothers and his father, and was walking in a daze, even as the first tourists of the day began to enter. They were visible only to other ghosts, and therefore in no danger, but still, this was not how he had envisaged his morning going.

Richard, George and their father halted in their tracks, steps behind Anne and Elizabeth. The former king looked to his brother, unsure how either of them would be welcomed, and hoping the usually-fun nature of George Plantagenet would come to the fore. Then again, this was also the first time all three brothers had been in the same place, alive or dead, for centuries: sibling rivalries and animosities could

93

run deep...

In the end, Jane Seymour broke the silence. Still the ultimate peacemaker, it would seem.

"Anne, it is so lovely to meet you," she said, stepping forward, carefully, between the two parties. "I know we haven't formally met, but I've heard so much about you from Anne of Cleves during our chats."

The referencing of their mutual friend, and their ongoing link since the Hampton Court visit, was clever, thought Richard. He almost replied with a reference to Anne Boleyn, before remembering where he was.

"Jane, you too. And of course, you will know your mother-in-law," replied Anne Neville, gesturing her niece forward. "Funny, so many of us still linked by our connections to that infamous husband of yours."

It was true, thought Richard, as he finally realised the men had remained silent for too long.

"Edward, it is good to see you," he said, forcing himself to make the first move.

Slowly, his elder brother's face seemed to melt from shock, to wearing the hint of a smile.

"Richard... I... I... Well, I don't know what to say," he said, his arms held open. "But Father, I am glad to see you, of that I can be absolutely certain." Closing the gap between them, Edward moved towards his father, and the two men embraced. "I'll never be sorry for being king, but I am sorry I never got to inherit the crown from you," he said, as they parted.

"At least you got it, son," the Duke replied. "Not many men can say they've sired more than one King of England, even if they never held the throne themselves."

Richard saw Edward tense at the Duke's vagueness over the mention of the throne, and his own dynasty, and wondered if his brother was also wondering whether the Duke's grandson counted in his number. To his relief, Hastings and George joined the huddle.

"So, Edward, as I said to them on the way here, it's been centuries, you must show us what has changed. And I want to see my own grave again." Hastings clapped his former sovereign on the back, and grinned.

"You shouldn't have left it so long. And yes, there have been plenty of changes."

"We should give you all the Grand Tour," said Jane, looking to Anne as though for confirmation of her plan.

"Hold on, hold on." The voice of Mary-Eleanor Bowes cut through the general murmurings of agreement. "Before we go gallivanting off, and risk not getting back here, I want to know if my great-grand-daughter is here."

"May we introduce Mary-Eleanor Bowes," said Richard, smiling at the lady in question.

"Bowes? Then you must of course be referring to the most wonderful Queen Elizabeth of them all, in our realm at least?" said Charles Brandon, chuckling at the scowl he received from Elizabeth Woodville as a result. He turned back to Mary-Eleanor. "The Queen Mother is here, but not here, my lady."

The whole group turned to him, questions on their faces.

"I mean to say this is where she generally resides, but she is currently in Scotland. Like her daughter, and as in her own lifetime, she enjoys part of her year visiting her other former residences: Glamis, May and Balmoral amongst them."

The slumping of Mary-Eleanor's shoulders caused Richard to step in before the day could be side-tracked. "You should speak to the Scots Queen. See if you can't steer her upcoming progress to fit in with the Queen Mother's plans, and then join her. A small holiday never does anyone any harm, after all." It was true enough; since he and Anne had started meeting up and travelling to places from their personal histories, he had been enjoying himself far more. He'd even been getting involved in more hauntings, much to the delight of his brother George.

"On with the tour then," cajoled Jane, moving to link arms with Charles Brandon, and steer their little party out into the sunlight.

"Funny to think all of us spent so much time here, across

the generations, and our descendants still do today, of sorts," mused Anne, as they meandered through the crowds and towards the main gate, Jane having decided they should follow the tourists' trail.

Richard watched a hint of sadness cross his wife's face. He knew it wasn't her own blood which ran through the veins of the current royals, in the same way that it wasn't his, but they both still felt the connection, and both were still undisputedly crowned King and Queen of England. He looked across at George, the pair of them one step behind the trio of Edward, the Duke, and Hastings. The reunion was always going to be a difficult one, but he truly wanted to find some sort of peace with his eldest brother. Even if it couldn't all happen today, some steps in the right direction would be a start.

As though sensing his gaze on her, Anne looked at Richard and smiled. He was about to say something, when Jane and Charles drew to a halt, indicating that the tour was about to begin.

"Now," said Brandon, "we are not averse to hauntings. With our history, heaven knows we have plenty of spirits, but there are a few ground rules we expect you, as visitors, to adhere to." He paused for effect, waiting for the group to nod their agreement, a smirk on his face. "It's rather satisfying, making monarchs and nobility agree to what you're telling them. But anyway, yes. This is an important historical site, as you are more than aware, and we get a lot of tourists, not all of which are up for the same level of haunting as they might be half-expecting at places like the Tower. Therefore, we request that any hauntings are kept within the limits of those already reported here. For example, we have Henry the Eighth loitering around St George's, which either myself or Edward usually take on. We also have Anne Boleyn. Yes I know," he said, reacting to Richard's scoffing laugh. "But the rumour is it's her, and that's what we go with. Jane or Elizabeth usually take on that role, and enjoy it, I believe. Other examples are Charles the First, although to be fair that sometimes really is him, there's the young lad in the Deanery, our horseman, the statues, and the young lass with the Christmas tree, although in her case she is more of a seasonal spirit, and won't be about just now. All of these are fine. As is the occasional glimpse of somebody in medieval or Tudor dress out of the corner of an eye, or the briefest reflection in a mirror or window. But anything beyond that, and there may be repercussions for all of us. Are we clear?"

All eyes turned to George Plantagenet.

"What?"

Charles didn't falter in his stare.

"Oh, fine, I'll behave. No excessive haunting."

"Very well then. Jane." He gestured for the former queen to take over, to the obvious disgruntlement of Elizabeth Woodville.

"He wants to watch it," George muttered to Richard. "Showing preference to anyone over the Woodville woman won't get him anywhere, even if it is to his own queen."

"Hush, man. Let's all just try and be civil, shall we? See if we can get something positive out of the day," Richard whispered back, before purposefully turning his attention to Queen Jane Seymour.

"Now, you'll of course know that a lot of what you see here today is actually part of reconstruction, undertaken in stages, with the current Round Tower based on what would have been here in the 12th century—"

"Jane." Edward cut in. "I'm sorry, we all know you have the tour learned by heart, but remember your audience. I think we can skip the history, and go for what's new?"

Momentarily flustered, Jane brushed imaginary creases out of her gown, then composed herself. "Of course, sorry. I can do modern, I can, I swear. Oh – the doll's house. That will be an excellent place to start, and then a tour of the royal apartments. How does that sound?"

Created in 1924 for Queen Mary (the wife of King George V), the doll's house was indeed the perfect beginning to things, as the group observed the London town-house in perfect period detail, before returning to the grand staircase to begin their tour of the Upper Ward.

Despite their best efforts, the visiting ghosts gasped as they confronted the armour of Henry VIII, at the heart of the Lantern Lobby. The Octagonal Room, more modern than any of their group, and only created after the 1992 fire, still managed to feel in keeping with the rest of the castle, especially having such a famous, or infamous, item at the heart of it.

"Were any of you here when fire struck?" asked Mary-Eleanor, glancing around the room, built in the area where the fire had begun.

"All of us," replied King Edward. "It was a terrible, terrible day for us all. We did hold a brief meeting, to see whether there was anything we could actually usefully do, but in the end, we just stayed well out of the way of everyone."

"It was heartbreaking to see," added Jane. "To watch your home go up like that."

"The effort to save everything was incredible," said Brandon. "And look around; you can see for yourself the quality of the restoration. That in itself is no mean feat, given the resources needed, and the skills at risk of being forgotten. Everything coming together like that was particularly impressive."

In truth, as the group meandered its way through the state and semi-state apartments, pointing out various rooms they had seen on television over the years, commenting on artwork of people or places they had known in life, and admiring the way the place managed to feel like both a palace and a fortress, there was little appetite for haunting. All they wanted to do was look around, catch up on old times where it was amicable, and tentatively try out new relationships and see whether there was the potential for them to last.

As they took a break from the bustle of the tourist crowds in the gardens below the Round Tower, Richard looked across at where his brother and father were once again deep in conversation. Likely reliving one of their great battles, or mulling over some big decision they had made together. It was strange, the four of them being back together. George had stayed near him all day so far, as though uncertain whether he should get too close to his father and elder brother. He had been quieter than usual, not even making the obvious jokes as they had walked through the Clarence Tower earlier in the day.

"We should try and say something, shouldn't we?" Richard asked his brother, nodding towards Edward and the Duke. "We've come all this way, put all this effort in, and seeing those two together, I don't know, it would seem a waste not to try."

"It's been civil enough so far, brother. Perhaps that's all we can hope for on a first visit," replied George.

He was right. There had been no heart-to-heart discussions, no deep conversations about their shared history, no brotherly talk about their past or future – but equally, there had been no animosity either. They had shared comments about art, conversed about the tourists that visited both Windsor and the Tower of London, and had been polite throughout, but there was no warmth. Stretching his neck from side to side as though limbering up for battle, Richard rose to his feet, and walked over to Edward and the Duke.

"Father, brother, I'm sorry to interrupt," he said, clearly interrupting, but unsure what else to do. He didn't like feeling unsure; he was looking forward to getting back to the Tower, where he had more control, where he felt more at ease. When things got out of hand there, like random locked-out teenagers, he could formulate plans, organise people, get things done. Here, he was feeling lost.

"Richard." Edward acknowledged him.

The Duke glanced between them both before speaking. "Come on now lads, we can do this, can't we? Can't you?"

The brothers looked at each other.

Richard spoke first. "I didn't expect us to become the

fastest of friends again in one visit, Edward. But I did hope that we could at least build a grounding, a foundation for something in the future."

"All the talk, Richard. What I heard, being here, what I saw. I came to London, you know. I was at your coronation." Edward held Richard's gaze, refused to blink.

Finally, Richard looked away. The coronation his brother would never believe was justified. That was their problem, and it was insurmountable as far as he could see. Perhaps their once-happy trio was too damaged to ever be truly reconciled.

At that moment, George strolled over, arm-in-arm with Queen Jane and Mary Eleanor, the latter immediately drawing the Duke into conversation. The quartet moved away, out of earshot, leaving the brothers alone.

"George never was great at subtlety," Edward said, half-smiling.

"We've given up trying at the Tower now; we just let him and Boleyn get on with it."

"Anne?"

"George."

"Ah. That sounds like it would be a challenging combination, from what I saw of George Boleyn."

"Oh, you have no idea. The pair of them keep us on our toes, believe me."

The thaw was starting, but would it ever really be enough?

"It's not easy, Richard, how could it be?"

Richard smiled. "It can't be. I know there's too much here, too many problems to get through."

"Far too many for one visit," agreed Edward. "But that's not to say that you shouldn't consider a second one."

"Really?"

Edward nodded. "It'll likely do all of us good to mingle more, clear the air, bit by bit. But she'll never be civil with you." He looked over at where his wife sat with their daughter, the two Elizabeths deep in conversation. "Our family history must be one of the most complicated in history, with all these interconnections, feuds and inherited hatred. But at least those two seem to be getting on well enough. Thank you for bringing her."

"She's a headstrong woman, your daughter, you know that. She'll always find a way of getting what she wants."

"Come, let's re-join the group and see if we can have a bit of fun this afternoon. We can't let you come all this way and not cause just a little bit of chaos."

"George got hold of a guidebook somehow – don't ask me how he got it into the rooms at the Tower – and he's quite keen to get into the Military Knights' Lodgings and see if he can't haunt a couple of the residents. And he definitely fancies getting back to Henry's armour and doing a bit of a 'flit' there. I think he was just a bit down in the dumps earlier." Richard looked across to George, now chatting to Mary-Eleanor, but glancing their way every so often.

"Oh, well, he deserves it. It's good to see him in a way, even after everything." He paused in their stroll back to the group. "This will take some time, Richard, and I'm fairly convinced that at some point in the future, I will again wish I could kill you, but for the sake of our father if nothing else, I'm keen to try. It's good to see him again."

Richard nodded. "It was a surprise to see him in York. You should see the display they have of his head in the Henry Tudor exhibition. Plastic, I mean. Horrid to come across it without warning."

"My head?" The brothers' father had turned to greet them, hearing the end of their conversation. "Yes, not the nicest thing. Turpin and Fawkes occasionally offer to let it befall some sort of 'accident' overnight, but I've told them to leave it be for now. It makes me chuckle that even in the middle of the Tudor exhibition, they have a reminder of the York family, even if it is a severed head."

"So?" George was also alert now, ready for the off. "A-haunting do we go?"

"Aye, brother, we do indeed, as long as we stick to Brandon's rules," replied Richard, laughing as George threw his arm around Hastings' shoulders and headed back towards the Upper Ward, already muttering about the best way to haunt a suit of armour.

Quietly, Anne Neville appeared at her husband's side. "Did that go as hoped? I saw you walk over to them."

"As expected, rather than as hoped, but it was fine. We have been formally advised that we may return."

"Well of course you may return; this was your palace just as much as it was Edward's; don't let him forget that. He isn't the only monarch in here, after all."

"No, and speaking of that, I wonder if Charles the First is around at all? It would be good to see him, and let him know how his son is getting on in Westminster." Richard tucked his wife's arm into the crook of his elbow, as their little party moved off.

"We'll ask Brandon when we get back to St George's, and see if he ever appears near his grave. If he does, then yes, that would be a good plan. For now though, let's go and see what trouble your brother decides to cause."

The 'trouble' George had in mind was tame compared to what he enjoyed at the Tower of London. Even without Brandon's warning, he knew that Windsor Castle didn't have the same reputation as the Tower; it was the same as with Westminster Abbey. In some places you might enjoy a little light haunting, but you couldn't really bring yourself to actually horrify anyone. And even in the Tower, they knew their limits.

He had second thoughts as they passed the Knights' Lodgings; there was really no point haunting the poor residents of the castle. In the same way as they tended not to irritate the Beefeaters and their families, giving any annoyance or anger to the people who were effectively their neighbours seemed unnecessary. But the Tudor fans gazing in awe at their favourite king's armour – they were a different matter entirely. Sensing that in Jane Seymour he had found a lady similar in nature to Jane Grey, George offered her his elbow as they approached the Upper Ward.

"Now, Your Grace, can I interest you in a walk on the Great Stair?" he asked, his words full of charm.

She glanced at him sideways, her face still for a moment, before breaking into a smile. "Now, what does the incorrigible Duke of Clarence have in mind for the stair, I wonder?"

"Nothing horrific. Brandon himself said that the slightest glimpse was enough. Might we just wait until there aren't many around, then make the briefest of appearances? They might even think we're the king and queen."

"I was the queen, if you remember," she said, squeezing his arm.

"Alright for some," he replied, pulling her up the steps just as a group of tourists entered the space. "Now, I know a little trick which we picked up from the Scots Queen."

It was a trick they had tried time and again now, one which was spreading like the proverbial hot cakes through all ghostly communities in need of an easy and not too terrifying haunt. Wait until a photo is being taken, and at the exact moment the button is pressed, flicker into full visibility, so that a fraction of appearance is captured.

"It's handy when they check the photo straight away," George commented, as they got into position. "But even if they don't pick up on what you've done until they're home, it's still a good giggle."

Jane tutted, but joined him in position as the group gathered, the two ghosts slipping easily to the back, behind four young women. The tallest member of the group reached out her arm, camera in hand, and snapped. With perfect timing, George and Jane glimmered into being, just a hint of Plantagenet and Tudor dress on show.

"I think we got it right," Jane whispered, "but did you see – it was one of those old-fashioned disposable things. She'll not find us until she gets home. Not a bad opener though. But come on, I have something more instant in mind."

Curious, he followed her through walls and corridors until they found themselves back at the doll's house.

"Ah… I think I can see where you're going with this," he

said, a grin on his face.

"Well, is there anything more creepy than toys moving? Now, there are two approaches here. First, is the family or group scenario. You wait until the first person in a group notices something of interest, then you gently move it whilst they turn away to point it out to somebody else. That's a fun one, as they are torn between keeping it to themselves, or sharing it with their friends, and risking looking daft."

"And second?"

"Second," continued Jane, "is for the solo visitors. For this, you need to be quick, and move something in such a way that it grabs their attention, but they don't actually see it move. Of course, being on their own, they're less likely to point something out to somebody else, or to speak to somebody if they see something weird, but equally, it's good fun because…"

"Because they can't get anyone else to back up what they have or haven't seen," finished George. "I like your way of thinking."

Richard, the Duke and Brandon were drawn to the doll's house room by the sound of confused gasps.

"He'd better not be causing bother," Brandon snarled at the Plantagenets.

"He won't be," retorted Richard.

"You would say that, wouldn't you? You're going to be loyal to your brother."

"Well, loyalty does bind me, after all. As it does you, I understand?" The fact that he and Brandon shared a motto had always amused him.

"Come on, you two. We'd better make sure Clarence hasn't actually destroyed the place whilst nobody was looking."

Richard grinned. The time with his father since the latter's arrival from York had been a positive experience so far. They had visited their old haunts in London, done a bit of reminiscing, and talked about so many things. It had been a rousing success, and one he hoped would repeat, especially if there was an invitation to revisit Edward too, after a decent interval. He laughed to himself as the Duke stalked on ahead of them. George was a fool at times, but he wasn't a total idiot; he wouldn't do anything to seriously endanger future relationships.

"If we come back, then I have the perfect idea for the Boleyns," George Plantagenet declared two hours later, as he finally walked away from the armour.

Anne Neville narrowed her eyes at him, then sighed. "Go on."

"Well, one of the ghosts here is meant to be Anne, yes, Tower Anne, Boleyn? So, why not get her over here, George too, and the two of them can 'become' Henry and Anne. A bit of a haunting domestic. It'll be hilarious!" He laughed as she tilted her head to the side, clearly considering his proposal. "Go on, you know she'll be up for it. Any chance to have a bit of fun at her ex-husband's expense. If not her, then Katherine Howard would surely go for it."

"He's right," said Richard, joining the pair. "She enjoys a good haunting. Especially if she's meant to be here anyway." He nodded at his brother. "Have a word when we get home; I think there's scope for more visits here in the future."

George grinned, knowing he would get his way and be able to have his fun.

By the end of the day, as the final tourists began to wind their way towards the exit, it was a tired but broadly contented group of ghosts which filed back into the choir stalls of St George's Chapel and took the chance to relax.

"I think that's been a mostly successful day," mused George, as he perched beside Elizabeth of York. "What did you think? Do I do a good performance of your monster of a son?"

"My son was not always the monster he is made out to be," the former queen retorted. "You know as well as I that in his youth he was the most perfect prince: handsome,

105

charming, intelligent, athletic…"

"A great husband." George ducked as his niece went to shove him in the ribs.

"Do not come to Westminster Abbey, Uncle George. I fear it would not end well for you. In fact, I promise that it would not end well for you."

"That's you told, brother. Do not anger my daughter. She was a magnificent queen," Edward IV said, smiling at his daughter.

At the back of the aisle, Richard and Anne had tracked down King Charles I, Brandon and Hastings were sharing tales of the highs and lows of true friendship with a ruling monarch, and the women were discussing the differences in their lives at the various palaces, then and now. As a distant clock struck five, the Duke rose to his feet and cleared his throat.

"Ladies, gentlemen, I know it's early still, but we might as well begin to make our way back into town and get home for the night, or at least to where we're calling home, temporarily. It has been a wonderful day for me, personally, and I would like to thank you all for making us so welcome, despite initial difficulties."

His words were echoed with a general murmur of agreement, as the visitors rose and began to make their individual farewells, knowing that with so much to say, it was likely to take a while.

In the chaos of the goodbyes, the promises not to leave things so long next time, and the plans for future visits to each other's ghostly homes, nobody noticed the extra shadow lurking in their midst, watching over events from the Queen's Closet, high above the floor of St George's Chapel. They never noticed him, and strangely, that had always been his choice. He knew full well what everyone – living or dead – thought of him, and he knew that despite the frequent annoyance of the ghosts he shared this place with, he was still at the forefront of their thoughts. He knew that even with recent royal weddings drawing attention, he was still the reason so many visited St George's, even if the grave he had been given wasn't exactly what he'd had in mind when he acquired those great pieces of marble, now moved to St Paul's to hold the body of Horatio Nelson.

He also knew that if he did ever reveal himself, he would once again be the centre of attention.

Then again, perhaps the time was drawing near when that might not be such a bad thing. He had heard of the meeting of his wives, and had seen their growing popularity over the centuries, and the way the story was changing. There was even a musical about them now, depicting them all as wronged superstars. He was no longer the romantic, heroic prince he had been; he was being turned into a monster, a bully, almost an object of derision. He couldn't be having that, could he? Even today, he had heard people talking about how his suits of armour had changed, how they could track the size of his waist, reference to the size of his stomach in later armour. That wasn't on. He was still a king; how dare he be overshadowed and mocked in such a way?

He would need to plan, to think this through carefully. He didn't want to simply appear one day out of the blue.

But, he decided, as the visiting ghosts went on their way, appear one day soon, he most certainly would.

THE END

Read the complete Kindred Spirits series:

Kindred Spirits: Tower of London

Kindred Spirits: Royal Mile

Kindred Spirits: Westminster Abbey

Kindred Spirits: York

Kindred Spirits: Ephemera

Fantastic Books
Great Authors

darkstroke is
an imprint of
Crooked Cat Books

- Gripping Thrillers
- Cosy Mysteries
- Romantic Chick-Lit
- Fascinating Historicals
- Exciting Fantasy
- Young Adult and Children's
  Adventures
- Non-Fiction

Discover us online
www.darkstroke.com

Find us on instagram:
www.instagram.com/darkstrokebooks

Printed in Great Britain
by Amazon